MW01279851

...GONE BUT NOT FORGOTTEN...

Jax March

Author's Tranquility Press
MARIETTA, GEORGIA

Jax March/Author's Tranquility Press
2706 Station Club Drive SW
Marietta, GA 30060
www.authorstranquilitypress.com

Publisher's Note: This is a work of fiction. Names, characters, places, and incidents are a product of the author's imagination. Locales and public names are sometimes used for atmospheric purposes. Any resemblance to actual people, living or dead, or to businesses, companies, events, institutions, or locales is completely coincidental.

Ordering Information:
Quantity sales. Special discounts are available on quantity purchases by corporations, associations, and others. For details, contact the "Special Sales Department" at the address above.

...Gone but Not Forgotten.../Jax March
Hardback: 978-1-958179-13-0
Paperback: 978-1-958179-14-7
eBook: 978-1-958179-15-4

A thousand words will never bring you home

I know because I have tried...

A thousand tears will never bring you home

I know because I have cried...

Contents

PROLOGUE

A little boy with his small face pressed up against the window overlooking the deck outside into the backyard. As he looked around he wondered "where were all the decorations? No cake? No presents" ...absolutely nothing. He felt awash with an overwhelming sadness. Everything that had led up to this day no longer mattered. today, you see was no ordinary day.

Today was Timothy Peterson's 6th birthday. A special age for him...he was no longer a quote-un-quote little kid. He was six and then meant no more pre-school. He was going to start "big kid" school. But nothing mattered to him at the moment because in his little mind everyone had forgotten. Or maybe they just didn't care?? With these somber thoughts running through his mind, he hung head down low and with his shoulders slumped he climbed the stairs to his room and put his favorite things in his backpack (the one he was supposed to use for school) and walked out the back door and disappeared...

We looked for Timmy, oh my god...miscommunication, Doug was supposed to take him this morning or so Faye thought...Faye was supposed to take him or so Doug thought...How could this happen? His presents remained unopened and soon a little six-year-old boy's birthday party was forgotten...As the panic set in and the police were called. It was supposed to be a surprise party but now there was no happiness just fear and unspoken dread...

Chapter I

$\mathbf{W}$hat a beautiful day Faye thought as she went about her business of making coffee and refreshments for all the mothers of the children that had attended Cassie's birthday party. As usual though Faye's mind would wander to a forgotten time. She would think back on a little boy's forgotten birthday that never happened. She thought to herself how different things would have been if only she had never left him alone that dreaded morning or if only Doug had taken him like he was supposed to. It was a bitter pill she swallowed every time something reminded her of that fateful day.

In Faye's mind Timmy had been taken...there was no other explanation, at least none that she could accept. In her heart she knew that someday her son Timothy would walk through her front door. Her family would be complete and it would be as if that terrible day almost eight years ago had never taken place. She smiled to herself when she imagined how handsome her son would be. He would be a man now not the cute little boy with tousled blonde hair and freckles.

The only way that Faye could deal with losing her baby boy was to imagine that some sweet barren couple had taken him out of desperation. She imagined that although what they did was a crime she knew that they loved him as if he were their very own. If Faye ever let herself believe anything differently or if someone said something different she would scream hysterically and burst into tears. It would take Doug hours, sometimes days to console her. She had to believe he was happy and alive, she just had to. As she rubbed the scars on her wrists to think otherwise was just not good.

In her own little world Faye relived that time over and over. There were more nights than not that she awoke with hot tears streaming down her face. The first few months after her son was taken were pretty much a hazy blur. She can remember bits and pieces of that time but not much else. All the questions from the Police, she even remembered the man-hunt and the search parties. All the people in and out of her house touching Timmy's things. This in and of itself felt wrong, an invasion of privacy in her mind. She kept silent though and let them do what she knew must be done. Self-blame was bad enough so when the police etc. blamed Faye and Doug. "Who leaves their six-year-old son home all alone?" A very difficult concept... who's to blame? Was it her fault? Was it Doug's? Was it fate? God's cruel trick? They say what doesn't kill you makes you stronger. This had definitely put that theory to the test. "Blame whomever you want Faye told them. Do what you must. Just find my son...please bring Timmy home."

When the blame game was finally over, the questions from the police began. First, they drilled Faye for what seemed like days...next was Doug. When they were finally convinced that the parents had made a mistake and had not purposely harmed their son. Then and only then the searching began. The noise, the dogs, the phone ringing non-stop with alleged sightings...It was too much and one day Faye had enough. It was just overwhelming, so she decided to steal a few moments to collect her thoughts. She couldn't do Timmy any good if she couldn't hear herself think. She stole away up to the bathroom to take a long hot bath and wait for the sleeping pills that Dr. Mills had prescribed to take effect. Before she even realized what she was doing it was done. She went from brushing her hair to shaving it all off. In her mind it was ok, with everything going on she had not had time to properly fix her hair...this was much easier. The more she shaved the calmer she became. Then a thought struck her like a bolt of lightning. Just maybe if she hurt herself the couple that had taken her son would sense it and feel bad and return him to her and Doug. Maybe they would realize what a terrible mistake they had made...just maybe? Before she could stop herself, she slid into the warm bath water and felt the release of the blade sliding across her wrists. Peace, it was ok...quiet.... it was ok...

By the time Doug found her, Faye was delirious and slipping in and out of consciousness. Her lips were turning blue and her skin was an ashen color. Doug was looking for her and when he opened the bathroom door, his legs gave out on him. What he saw drained all the blood from his face and made him physically ill. At first, he wasn't sure what he was looking at, there was hair strewn all over the bathroom sink and the floor. It was as if he was in a horrible dream. Finally, when the shock wore off, he realized that there in the bathtub was his beautiful wife laying in what he could only describe as deep red wine. As he knelt by the bathtub and gingerly scooped her out of the water and cradled her to him...Faye looked up at him and though her voice was not more than a whisper at this point she calmly said, "Don't worry sweetheart, you'll see...now they'll bring our little boy home to us, they know..." With that a weak smile played across her lips and Faye was gone.

Chapter II

When Faye woke up, she was extremely disorientated. At first, she looked around frantically having no idea where she was. When her eyes adjusted and she took in the sterile surroundings, she realized she was in a hospital and her first thoughts went to Timmy. What on earth was going on? Did they find Timmy? Faye tried to sit up...she had to know, but "what's going on? Why can't I sit up? Why am I in a hospital bed? I can't move?" Faye turned her head and saw the nurse at the foot of her bed and asked why she was here? It was then out of the corner of her eye she noticed Doug; he was leaning against the sill staring aimlessly out of the window. He looked worn out and the furrows in his brow looked almost painful. His clothes were all disheveled...Why does he look so worried? It must be Timmy, Faye thought. Why isn't anyone talking to me? What's going on? Where is my son? Faye tried to speak ...Faye tried to voice her fears, why couldn't she speak? Oh God, that pesky nurse is still by the foot of the bed, w- wait a minute what is she saying...? "Mrs. Peterson...oh good there you are, back with us. We almost thought we'd lost you. Don't try to Speak right now, we have given you a slight sedative so that you wouldn't be agitated when you woke up. If there is anything I can get for you later don't hesitate to ask there will be a nurse present at ALL times." With that, she smiled and walked to the edge of the room and sat down looking over her chart. I tried to speak to Doug... "Doug, Doug what's going on? Why am I here? Doug, Doug...what happened...hard as I try, I can't remember and nothing is making any sense". All that came out was a weak moan. Doug didn't move, he couldn't hear me. "Maybe" I thought, "the words were just in my head?" A doctor, finally someone that will know what's going on...I was very happy to see Dr. Mills walk into my room. I tried to ask... where is he going? I'm here I tried to say... His focus was not on me. He is acting as if I'm invisible... confusion washed over me. Everyone is talking over me...am I here? Am I dreaming? I'll try to get his attention; it's then I realize that I can't move my arms, I can't sit up...why? I'm in restraints, I'm so confused. I mouthed the words, but nothing came out. They then put the syringe into my IV. Everything again went dark, and the peace once again washed over me...

In my dreams I'm always with Timmy. His smile and giggles are infectious. Such a happy little boy. Not a care in the world. He was so excited to start school in a few months. We made such plans, he made me promise that I would be one of those moms that attended every field trip – this is one promise that I intended to keep. I wanted to be that mom. He diligently studied all his numbers and letters. I think he was harder on himself than anyone else was. He was so excited to go to school, everyday he'd ask, "is it time yet? Is school starting yet?" A perfectionist like his Father. I saw so much of Doug in Timmy...the way they walked, the things they said. Even when they watched TV together, they both had pillows nestled in their laps and each had a slight head slant. You didn't notice it unless you really knew them. It was quite funny the simple things you notice when you love someone. If ever there was a "mini-me" it was Timmy. He had such a wonderful life ahead of him. It was amazing to see the world through my son's eyes. My dreams were a happy place I hated to wake up...reality came crashing in much too quickly. Timmy was gone.

Chapter III

(Doug's story)

"Faye...Faye where are you? We got a good lead on Timmy to...Oh my God! Mom, Mom call 911...hurry its Faye...shhh-she oh my God mom just call 911!!!" Oh Faye, honey what have you done? Why didn't you talk to me? You seemed to finally be coming to terms with the possibility that Timmy might not come home. At least I thought you did...hold on a second honey, "What mom? Send them up...huh? What? Faye did you say something?" I almost dropped her when she peacefully uttered those words...What did she mean, "they'll bring our boy home now?" I couldn't lose Faye not after losing Timmy. To walk into the bathroom and see my wife's beautiful limp body lying almost lifelessly in a tub of dark red blood and see her gorgeous blonde curls carelessly strewn all over the sink and the floor. Faye was always so meticulous I just couldn't believe what I was seeing. My legs gave out on me as I slid down the side of the tub. All I could think was, "oh my God my entire family, my reason for living was gone." First Timmy and now my beautiful Faye was... Wait...Faye is alive!

At the hospital they put her on suicide watch. Dr. Mills is explaining to me how close we came to losing her. He says don't worry about outward appearances, her hair will grow back and while there will be scars her wrists will heal. It's her mental state that we need to worry about. People that try once and don't succeed usually try again. In these circumstances we'll have to be extra diligent. "I'll talk to her when she wakes up and access her then," Dr. Mills said. "Once we've determined her state of mind, we will know better how to treat her."Dr. Mills continued to talk...something about a 24-hour nurse blah blah blah. All I could do was look over at my sleeping wife, she looked so peaceful now. I wonder how in the world we ever ended up here? My beautiful Faye laying in the hospital bed she looked so fragile, and I let her down. It was my responsibility to take care of her and keep her safe...I have failed her miserably. I wasn't there when she needed me the most. This will never happen again. Whatever Faye needs I will be there and I will do it...Never again!

Chapter IV

I closed my eyes and remembered a time when we were so very happy. A time when we didn't have a care in the world. We were newlyweds – me struggling through my last year of Medical School and Faye...ah beautiful Faye, she was the prettiest little Candy-Striper I had ever seen. Long blonde hair, dimples...the prettiest blue eyes. The first time I saw her I felt it, I just knew that she would become the most important person in my life. I felt such a fierce need to shelter and protect this delicate flower. Whenever I saw some other guy giving her attention, I felt a jealousy such as I had never felt before.

But I knew when she smiled at me it was ok. I was her guy, her one and only and no one would ever come between us. I knew she would mother my children. I knew she was my soulmate. And without a doubt I knew that for the rest of our lives there would never be anyone else for me. This is the woman that would make the bad time bearable, the good times the best and all the times in between just as memorable. We could go out; we could stay in...as long as we were together it just didn't matter.

We had a whirl-wind courtship and we married within the first year and even through all the heartache I have never once regretted my decision. Everything I have become and everything I have done has been for Faye and then for Timmy...I never thought that two people that have so much love for each other would or could share so much tragedy. My beautiful little boy who somehow has been snatched out of my aching arms. You never really know what love is until you hold your child in your arms for the first time. Now there is a hole in my heart that I don't know how to heal.

Faye had a difficult pregnancy, but she never complained. We were so worried; Faye was so careful. She took excellent care of herself. Through all her discomfort she never looked so beautiful to me as she did then. She was so excited to become a mother. She read so many books on pregnancy...she played classical music and laid the headphones on her growing belly. When she felt the baby kick for the first time, she called everyone we knew. Although it was rough and she was sick more than not it was the most precious time we ever experienced. It brought us so close. I thought about her carry my child and I would swell with such pride and more love then I knew I could possess. And then when Timmy was born, he was perfect. I felt like the king lion, pride and protection and love took over my every waking thought. I think I called her at least 100 times per day. I wanted to know every little move that Timmy made. I had to work and being away from my little family was the most difficult thing I had ever had to experience...at least that's what I thought. I was never so determined to take care of and provide for my family...We had the perfect life. Timmy would want for nothing – but we would make sure that he was kind and loving. He would grow up and appreciate everything he received. But, most of all Timmy would never doubt the love that Faye and I had for him. I had such plans for him. Faye and I grew together with so much love for our little family. Our life was perfect. Your children are the best part of each of you rolled into one person. With that in mind Timmy would make a difference in so many people's lives no matter what he did.

There was another very important person in Timmy's life that made a huge impact on him. That person is my mother. This is the woman who was always so stern with me growing up. Dad died when I was very young, so it was just my mom and myself. She had to be both mother and father. I never realized what a responsibility that was until we had Timmy. As a parent you have the job of shaping your child into the adult that they are to become. She was tough but she was my best friend. When I had a bad day, she knew and a comforting squeeze of my shoulder told me everything I needed to know without ever a word being uttered. Mom worked two jobs but never missed any important event in my life. Ball games, proms, award ceremonies...and anything else that I needed her to attend. We never had much money, but we had a lot of love. Having to be both mom and dad though, she was hard on me. She wanted me to be the best person I could possibly be. Mom went through cancer and worked two jobs and went to school. She came up from nothing and made something of herself. With that in mind if there was a major issue she was always in my corner. But there was no feeling sorry for myself and a can't do attitude was a big no-no. Her philosophy was simple, "when you are at your weakest point and feel like you can't go on that is when your inner strength emerges, and you find out exactly what you are made of." I was always in awe of my mom and so very proud of her she made me want to push myself to meet and surpass each and every goal I set for myself. Hard yet soft...loving yet stern. She was my rock; she was my knight in shining armor. She was my best friend until Faye.

When Timmy came along, I saw such a change in my mom, she opened up to this little boy. She loved him with every breath in her body. They went everywhere together. Believe me when I say the feelings were mutual. When Timmy saw his Oma his little face lit up like a Christmas tree, it was amazing to watch. Timmy loved his Oma, she was his best friend. They would whisper and giggle and no one but the two of them would have known or had a clue what the joke was about. The day Timmy disappeared I saw a light go out in mom's eyes. It was like looking back into the past to the day dad passed away. Oh, at first mom thought like everyone else did that Timmy was taken. Somehow, she believed we would get him back, a possible ransom note? He wandered off? No one thought for one minute that he was just gone never to return...surely not? Right? Slowly as the days turned into weeks and the weeks into months mom knew, deep in her heart she knew Timmy was gone. Now she and Faye hardly spoke. Mom is a realist and, in her mind, Faye needed to accept the fact that our sweet boy was somehow dead. If he were alive, he would have found a way to come back home to us.

Me, well I was just numb, I threw myself into my work. I guess in the recesses of my mind I thought every time I saved a life, some other doctor somewhere might be doing the same for my son. Or maybe the reason, the real reason was that I couldn't bear to go home and put on the façade for Faye's sake that Timmy was alive and was going to come home any day. How could I tell her that deep down in the pit of my stomach I knew something was terribly wrong. How could I look in those beautiful blue desperate searching eyes and tell her that our son was dead and would never return. I couldn't do it, I plastered a fake smile on my face and pretended. When I couldn't pretend, I threw myself into my work. Somehow cutting people open and sewing them up had become my sanctuary.

...I'll see you someday thinks a mother to her son

In the future not so near she sighs with a tear

Until then my sweet child I will always love you

From here

A place in my heart where we are never apart...

Chapter V

(The Homecoming)

After a few months in the hospital and then almost seven months at Meadow View Psychiatric Clinic (one of the best in the country) we brought Faye home. She was quiet and withdrawn. She had lost a lot of weight. When she looked at you, she always had a faraway look now. She reminded me of one of those abused animals that forget how to trust. She was a shell of the woman she had been. She was in total denial, and we were told that it was her minds way of protecting her from the pain. So at first, we were told to play along and that eventually when she was mentally strong enough her mind would let her accept the whole ugly painful truth. Until then though the fantasy lived that someday Faye would hold her young son in her arms. That she would once again rock her baby to sleep in her arms until he drifted off. So, we played along. My mom moved in so that there was always someone at home with Faye in case reality came crashing in and she couldn't deal with it. I wanted someone there to hold her and let her know that we could and would survive this terrible time.

What about me, you ask? Like I said I had thrown myself into my work. If someone couldn't come in, I took the shift. Holidays, I was there too. I worked as much as I possibly could and when I had to go home, I played Faye's game the rest of the time. That is how my life went, "the calm before the storm."

Time stood still in our house. It was no longer a home, it was just a constant reminder of what once was. Faye never let us move to a new house because she was afraid that when Timmy was able to, he wouldn't know where to go. We received so many crank calls and people wanting to know how we could leave our son at home alone. People were very hurtful and rude. But even the ones that had the best intentions were a nuisance. I believe in God just like the next person but it is very hard to even try to put something like this behind us and have some type of life when everyone is constantly dredging it up. I didn't want to forget my son, it's just sometimes I resented his memory. It hurt too damn much and I was never allowed to put him to rest. Faye talked about him as if he were just at school and would be home any minute. At first when she set the table for meals there was always a place setting for Timmy. It got to the point where Faye ate alone with her memories and mom and I ate elsewhere with our nightmares. There was more...Faye insisted that we not change our phone number because she had made sure that Timothy knew his address and phone number (in case he ever got lost.) So, if we changed either he would not have any idea how to contact us if the chance ever arose. It was like walking on eggshells and hoping that none of them would break. It felt as if our life was at a standstill, we were living in Faye's make-believe world. I didn't know how long I could do this...hell I didn't know much of anything anymore. Faye had a delicate grasp on reality, so we were all very careful in what we said or did around her.

Chapter VI

(Edna's story)

I love my son, when he was very young his father passed away so it was always just he and I. I was hard on him but that was only so that he would be the best man he could. We didn't have a lot of money when he was young, I worked two jobs to help make ends meet. We had trials and tribulations that we went through. Money, health issues...I don't like to dredge up the past, lord knows we live it every day now with the Faye situation. Suffice to say there were struggles but we lived modestly and Doug and I made it through. I do love Faye, when Doug brought her home for the first time, I knew he was smitten. I had not seen him that happy in a very long time. Although I thought they were rushing into it they married quickly. I knew that theirs was a love that would last a lifetime...Faye and Doug would be married until the time came that they just weren't anymore. They would be together until death did them part. When people saw them together you couldn't help but smile. She brought out the boy in him and he brought out the best in her. A match made in heaven, I couldn't have chosen better for him had I had the choice. Shortly after their honeymoon they told me the news...Faye was expecting. Oh my...I had just gotten used to having a daughter and now I was going to be an Oma...Wow, life was about to change. Not mine but definitely Doug and Faye's for sure.

Was I ever wrong! On the day my beautiful grandson was born it was like a ray of sunshine on a cloudy day. He melted my heart with every little smile, his tiny fingers wrapped around my thumb. All I wanted to do was protect him from anything and everything that might ever hurt him. We were more than grandson and grandmother; we were best friends. We went everywhere together. We did everything together...we were inseparable. I made sure to see or talk to him every day. I was there when Timmy rolled over, sat up and ate solid food for the first time. His first tooth is in my jewelry box. When we cut his hair for the first time it was Oma that held his hand. With his chubby little legs, it was Oma he wobbled over to. We visited the park and fed the ducks daily, played in the rain puddles...Every night it was Oma that read his goodnight story either in person or over the phone. But then my world came crashing down. I had just spoke to him that morning. I wanted so much to tell him that I hadn't forgotten his "big boy birthday." He and I went wish shopping and he had picked out a bicycle. So many questions about the bicycle. He was so inquisitive and so smart...My boy would go far in his life! Oma would make sure of that. Christmas's were special for us. I would go pick him up and we drove around the neighborhoods and gawked and oohed and ahhh'd at all the decorated houses and yards.

Tradition...we stopped and got hot chocolate with marshmallows to drink while we had our adventure. I knew that when he got older and had a family of his own, he would do the same with his children. Money isn't everything, making memories for and with the ones you love makes life worth living.

The day that Timmy disappeared I felt as if my life was over. I was sure I was the last person he spoke with. When I talked to him, I had a feeling that something was wrong with him. I wish I had questioned him more. Maybe it would have made a difference? Were the kidnappers there with him? Is that why he sounded so funny and distraught? I'll never know, but I should have known. I knew something was wrong, I should have listened to my sixth sense and gone to the house. I should have asked to speak to Faye or Doug? It seemed kind of strange to me that Timmy answered the phone. So many things I could have done but didn't do. Maybe it would have made a difference? Blame is a funny thing. We had been planning his surprise birthday for months and in the back of my car I had a shiny blue bicycle with a helmet and knee pads and the works. I pictured Timmy learning to ride his new bike. What do I do with it now? Can't make myself give it away. Where are you Timmy?

When Faye went into the hospital my heart broke for her, there was nothing I could do to help her. I always thought that it is an unnatural state of affairs for a parent to lose a child – how do you fill that void? I don't think I could have survived losing my son. I was grieving myself and here was Faye being needy and it made me angry with her. Right or wrong I thought she should be strong, Doug needed her to be strong not fall apart. He was going through enough and now this. But I think I was the angriest because like Doug my life would end too if we had lost Faye. She was being weak and I needed to know that she was strong and able to cope not only for my sake but for Doug's sake as well.

Prior to Faye becoming pregnant with our Timmy, she had lost a baby. She was almost in the third trimester so she could already feel the baby kick and move around. We had thrown her a baby shower so she and I had the nursery decorated, it was ready and waiting. One night there had been a horrible storm and we lost all the electricity. On this fateful night Faye was going down the stairs and one of the windows blew open and "whoosh" out went the candle she was holding and her nightgown got wrapped around her legs...down she went. The fall down the stairs was bad but when she hit the ceramic tiled landing she ended up with a concussion and she also lost the baby. It was horrible, she didn't lose the baby right away. It actually took a few days for the terrible ordeal to transpire. You see, because of the concussion Dr. Mills insisted on keeping Faye overnight at the hospital. We were relieved because that way the baby could also be monitored. All seemed ok, naturally when Faye came home, she was in quite a bit of discomfort. We all assumed the pain was from the fall, we believed that until the cramping and bleeding started. Dr. Mills ended up having to perform a partial birth abortion. The baby had expired and we did not want infection to set in. We lost our baby girl, Dr. Mills assured us that Faye was healthy and would be able to bear more children. When Dr. Mills delivered her, she was so tiny but oh so beautiful. We christened her Catherine and had a small service and burial for her. Poor Faye it was times like these that I know how much she wished her mother was still alive. I love Faye, she is the daughter I had never had. I know had her mother been here she would have been able to cope with the situation much better. I feel that in certain circumstances, and I don't care what they are, separating a child or children from their mother it makes coping with difficult times that much tougher. Since Faye was a loner and didn't have many friends it was up to Doug and myself to see her through this while coping with the loss ourselves. Doug and I were the only family that Faye had. That little girl, our Catherine was going to mean the world to her. It wasn't meant to be. So, while the funeral was going on I had someone go over to Doug and Faye's home and pack up all of little Catherine's clothes and belongings and take them to Goodwill or somewhere like that. After that Catherine's name was never mentioned again. At least never in Faye's presence. She is such a delicate person and Doug fretted over her so. Faye always blamed herself for what happened to Catherine. Just as now she blames herself for Timmy. By all accounts I feel we are all to blame for what happened to

Timmy. Still to this day though we have no idea what happened.

I do know that Timmy and I had such a close bond that whenever I go over to Doug and Faye's house, I feel his presence. It's almost like he's there or very very close by. Sometimes the feeling is so strong I feel a shudder run up and down my spine. If I close my eyes, I can feel Timmy's small hand in mine. If I turn around, I can swear he'll be there, "Oma, Oma come see what I did!" I can almost feel him tugging on my shirt. Of course, he never is there...wishful thinking on my part, I guess. On other occasions I swear I can hear him calling out to me. There are days that I can't stand being there. But I am drawn to the house, Timmy is there if only in spirit...I know he is.

After we brought Faye home from Meadow Hills Doug asked me to move in with them. While Faye was away, I practically lived there anyway. I watched my son go from happy to morose. Right before my eyes he aged at least 10 years. No smiles, no laughter, it's as if we were just going through the motions. Doug was like a robot, get up go to the hospital then come home. Eat his meals in silence, half the time I don't think he even knew what he was eating. Nothing really mattered to him. The weekends were the worst, those were the days he didn't have any excuses to go to work. So, he had to put a fake smile on his face and live in Faye's fantasy world. It was not really living just surviving, biding time really. I worry about both Faye and Doug. My son is strong, but even the strong can only take so much. When he walks in from work and finds Faye straightening up Timmy's room it breaks his heart. Or other times when she comes home from a shopping spree and has new items for Timmy because in her mind, he has outgrown all of his clothes. Doug feigns enthusiasm as Faye's eyes sparkle when she shows him the new clothes or shoes or whatever it is. Poor thing he tries so hard to share her hope. Inside though he just wants to crawl in a hole and never come out. Can she not see what she is doing? Faye is living in a bubble and eventually it will burst. I still wonder if we are doing the right thing. Shouldn't she face it and then let the healing begin? There have been so many times that I just want to shake her and make her wake up but as of yet she is living in an imaginary world. Holidays are the worst by far. For Christmas Faye plans a big dinner and buys all kinds of presents for me and for Doug and just as many for Timmy. It never fails though, every year when all the celebrating is done, and the only presents left under the tree are Timmy's for a brief moment reality hits Faye and she runs upstairs and locks herself in her room and cries for hours. Poor Doug takes the tree down and just sits and stares at the fire and never says a word. Something had to change, I'm not sure what but I did know that this couldn't go on indefinitely. I decided that when I took Faye for her next evaluation I was going to sit down with the doctors and make them tell Faye the truth. The evaluations started out once a week. It was hard for Faye but she did it. Soon though they went to once a month. I think sometimes the doctor's fix the symptoms and never face the problems that cause them. We have to be able to weather the storm when we still have the strength to do it. Yes, I felt a kind of peace...Faye's next appointment would be the awakening that she needs. it would be the healing that we have all put on hold. It won't be what we planned but it will be a new beginning. A new kind of normal awaited us all. But as usual things change...

Chapter VII

(A Surprise)

There is joy in our house again, could it be? Faye is beaming from ear-to-ear. "Edna...call Doug, he needs to come home immediately! I need him home now!" confused, I asked her ..." What's going on child?" I asked her as I dialed Doug's number. When she told me I dropped onto the couch in shock and disbelief. Can this be real? When Doug answered, in a shaky voice I could barely get the words out... "c-come home son, come home now." I could still hear Doug's voice in the phone as it slid out of my hand onto the floor. I could hear his frantic words..."Mom, mom... what's wrong? Is it Faye?" I just sat there in shock and disbelief unable to move. The phone went dead and I knew he was on his way. Stay safe my son...just come home I mouthed into the dead air.

Doug jumped into the car. Although he flew home the drive seemed to take forever. So many thoughts were racing through his head. Did she try it again? Is she alright? If she had tried to end her life, why did mom call me? He started to get angry as he pulled into the driveway and threw open the door and the look of fear and worry on his face was just too much...Soon his fear turned to confusion, Faye was in the kitchen flitting around and singing. I was still sitting on the couch in disbelief. Doug just stood in the middle of the living room looking around. Finally, he found his voice, "will someone please tell me what is going on? Please, mom? Faye?" I just pointed to the kitchen and Doug made his way there.

Doug entered the kitchen and Faye was beaming. "Doug, we are having a baby!" Doug found the nearest chair and fell into it. "Are you sure? How? When?" Faye proceeded to tell him that she was a little over three months along. Doug could hear her talking but he was lost in his own thoughts...all he kept hearing was, "we're having a baby." Then it finally registered... "Oh my God! We're having a baby!" Oh wow, there were a million questions running through my head. Maybe just maybe we were meant for Happiness after all?

The joy was short lived, once again there were complications, and our happiness was over before it began. Pre-Eclampsia is what they said. It was kind of a blur, after that I just kind of gave up. It was as if our family was cursed. At least this time it happened quickly. We christened this child Brandon. Yes, it was a little boy. It had been too soon to see any real features, but he was ours and he was loved. Faye seemed to go numb after Brandon died. She sat in her Grandmother's old rocker in the baby's room for what seemed like hours every day and softly sang as she looked out the window. She clutched the new teddy bear and she imagined many times giving it to our child to soothe his or her cries. An empty aching feeling overtook me. I never showed it, I had to be strong for Faye and mom. But I felt it. I worried about Faye, she seemed to retreat inside herself. She never mentioned the baby as a matter of fact she never talked much at all these days, she simply rocked and sang and stared out into space as tears made their way down her beautiful porcelain face. I wondered if this time if she tried to end her pain if I would stop her or let her go? Would I keep her here for me or let her be with our children? That was a stupid thought and I quickly dismissed it from my mind. Children or no children we had each other and maybe that's how it was meant to be? I didn't understand it, but I could accept it if only Faye would smile. How I missed her sweet smile and her laugh. The sound of her laughter used to fill our home. If I concentrated hard enough, I can still hear it echoing through the halls. I vowed I would do whatever it took to hear her laugh again.

Those we love ne'er go away

They live in our hearts each and every day.

Gone but not forgotten that where they are

Their spirit lives within you

Forever as your heart.

Chapter VIII

(Oma Gets Sick)

Doug and I tried to make Edna comfortable in her last few months with us. When I lost the baby, she seemed to lose her will to live. This strong woman looked so feeble, and my heart broke for her. On the nice warm days, I take her out on the back deck that overlooks the gullies and then the forest. Edna loves to come out here, she worries me though because she often sits in her wheelchair and holds lengthy conversations with Timmy. She laughs and she cries. I cry for her because it seems her mind is going quicker than her body can deteriorate. Edna seemed to get sick shortly after I lost the last baby. She seemed to catch a cold and it just never got any better. After many doctor visits it was as if she had just given up. Now we keep her as comfortable as we can because we both know that the end will come soon for her. She spends her days on the deck talking to who she insists is Timmy and her nights are spent in fitful sleep. On the colder days when she can't go outside, she just sits quietly by the window that overlooks the back deck and holds her hand up as if she is trying to let someone or something know she is still there. She often tells me, "Faye, he's scared and wants to come home but doesn't know how to." Those simple words haunt me still. It used to bother me that she would talk as if my Timmy was dead, but now it's just the ramblings of an old woman and I accept it. Timmy is not dead...He will come home. Doug comes home earlier from work now; he tries to coax his mother away from her perch by that window. It doesn't work and just agitates poor Edna and makes Doug feel useless. She eats very little these days so we know the end will be soon.

Then one day it did come, death came and stole Edna away while she was napping on the back deck. It was swift and painless. I went in to get her some warm tea because it was pretty cold out that day. I tried to get her to stay in but she insisted on being outside. When I brought her the tea her breathing was shallow. I went in to grab the phone and call Doug but she grabbed my hand and asked me to sit with her. The last word I heard Edna speak was, "Timmy." She brought her feeble hand to my cheek gently stroked it and then our Enda was gone. In our short lives Doug and I had lost so many loved ones. We lost Catherine, Timmy, and our last the last baby Brandon. Now we had lost Edna. She was the closest thing I had to a mother. We didn't see eye-to-eye on a lot of things, and I know that I was a disappointment to her. But I loved her still and I'll love her until the end. We were almost afraid to wake up in the morning wondering what will come next. Death seemed to be a sweet release from the pain anymore. Of course, I'd never say that to Doug. But sometimes I yearn for it. Sometimes I just wanted to give up the fight and just let go. I didn't because I knew my husband would be ashamed of me and he would blame himself. Doug is so strong; I don't know how he does it? He always tries to make me laugh. The few times I do it sounds so hollow and foreign to me. It's as if it is a stranger's voice I hear and not my own.

When Edna passed, Doug seemed to take it in stride. It's a bad thing when death doesn't affect you like it should anymore. He went through the steps almost mechanically... the funeral, the burial and then it was done. If he mourned for his mother, he did it in silence. I was too caught up in my own world to notice the lines that were permanently etched in his brow. I was too preoccupied to notice the faraway look he had and the tears threatening to spill down his cheeks. I didn't notice that he barely came to bed and when he did, he slept maybe an hour or two. Maybe it was my way of coping...the oblivion and numbness. The world around me did not exist. The only reality I knew was my safe haven...my house. This is where Timmy would come home to. Little by little I found excuses to never leave. Oh, I justified my reasons, what if no one was home when my son came or no one was here to answer the phone when he called. Life had been cruel to us but we were each strong in our own way. Besides Timmy was not dead...I wouldn't accept that. If Doug noticed the change in me he never said anything. He did what Doug does, he just accepted it as another part of his life. We never went out and no one ever came to visit accept one.

First, he came out of duty but then he came out of the goodness of his heart.

When Timmy disappeared, we always had police stopping by. Officer Jess, one of the nice ones that used to stop by on a regular basis only comes by from time-to-time now. I used to think it was out of pity or duty but then it became a real friendship. We often got into what I called were arguments, but he said they were a difference of opinion. He would try to convince me that there was no evidence that Timmy was alive... I always came back with, "well there is no evidence that he is dead either!" At that Officer Jess would just put his hand on my shoulder, give it a knowing squeeze, get up, sadly shake his head and say his goodbyes and leave. I wonder what he thinks. Sometimes, not often though he would stop in just to check on us. When Doug was at work, he stopped by to see if I was ok. He noticed and questioned me as to why I never left the house. My explanation didn't sit well with him. Training had taught him though that people have different ways of coping with tragedy and he guessed this was mine.

Besides Officer Jess no one really comes around anymore. If Doug gets an invite to a hospital function he politely bows out because he knows I won't go. My rational is simple, if we are gone and Tim were to come home, well then there would be no one home. I make sure there is always someone home...always.

And so went our life. The few friends we had quit coming by and the phone quit ringing. The visits from the police became further and further apart. People kind of forgot we existed. I liked it this way. I am sure the sensationalism will start up again when my son reappears. All the doubters and the nay-sayers will eat their words. And my Doug will smile again. My family will be complete and life will be good. I just have to hold on, some days' fly by while others are spent crying into my pillow. With Edna gone there is no one to talk to. Doug is never here anymore. I long for the laughter...

Chapter IX

The hospital has become Doug's safe haven and our home became mine. I never drove anywhere anymore hell I never left the house. Somehow it just became the norm, Doug did all the shopping. The change just kind of snuck up on us. I don't think either of us really paid attention to it. We were both so caught up in trying to cope that we forgot how to live. It started with the little things, someone always had to be home. With Edna gone that fell to me. I couldn't even bear to walk down the drive to the mailbox – what if the phone rang and no one answered? What if it was Tim? I had figured out how long it took to get from room to room so that I never missed a phone call. It just simply got to the point that one day I just never left the house again. At first, I don't think Doug even noticed, when he finally figured it out he would try and coax me out. Not even on the front porch – I wouldn't be able to get to the phone in time if it rang. He tried so hard to get me to come and at least swing with him on the back deck...I couldn't. For some reason when I would try to appease him and attempt it, I broke out in a cold sweat and got extremely sick to my stomach. I would lose all the strength in my legs and try as I might I just couldn't step out past the glass sliding doors that in my mind protected me from all the terrible things that lurked outside. Whomever took my son lived out there. I was safer in here and perfectly happy to stay safe and sound in my haven. I never missed going outside. No one could ever hurt me if I never left my house.

Doug tried to make things as easy as possible for me. He put a mail slot in our front door so I could look through the mail prior to him getting home. At least I was able to contribute a little bit in that sense. If Doug had to work late which he did often he called me every hour to make sure that I was alright. He even got me a cell phone in case I wanted to go outside. It also worked if there was a snowstorm or some other catastrophe that Mother Nature threw our way. At this point we were pretty much immune to disappointment and pain. Our life was pretty mundane. No excitement, staying in my house was a very satisfying life for me. The only thing I missed that would complete my life was if my son walked through my door. Someday I knew that would happen. It had been 4 years now since Timmy was taken. He would be 10 years old now. It is hard for me to wrap my head around that thought. I wonder how much he looks like his father now? Does he play sports? What type of movies does he like? Let's see...hmmm, 10 no I don't think he'd like girls yet. If he looked anything like his dad they'd be flocking around soon enough. Maybe I'd make a few phone calls and have one of those sketch artists take a baby picture and make me a portrait of what my son looks like now. Maybe the next time Officer Jess comes to visit I'll ask him if the police sketch artist could do that for me. We could place the picture above the fireplace. It would feel as if Tim is home. My son is still alive in this house and to gaze at his portrait would warm up even the coldest days. Yes, that is what I'll do. He'll come home someday and know that even though he hasn't been here he was never forgotten. It will make the waiting a little more bearable. Out of sight but never out of mind and always close to my heart.

A few days later my plans came to fruition. Officer Jess took one of the last pictures I had of Timmy to give to his buddy who happened to be the police sketch artist and asked him to do this for me. It took a few weeks but was well worth the wait. When he brought me the picture I was so nervous. He quietly slipped the package into my hands and left. I guess he knew that this unveiling was something I needed to do on my own and alone. As I unwrapped the plain brown paper what emerged made me drop to my knees. My beautiful baby was no longer a baby. I already knew this in my heart but to see it staring you in the face was a sharp bite of reality. It was bittersweet, the face staring back at me was no longer round and chubby. He still had his dimples and his blonde wavy curls and I knew him right away, but he was a young boy now almost a teenager. Reality hit hard, I gazed at his pictures for what seemed like hours. I dawned on me how much of Timmy's life I had missed. Sadness and joy enveloped me at the same time. For the first time I actually wondered if my boy would recognize me? Had he forgotten us? He was so young when he was taken from me. I never forgot, I could tell you where every scrape and bruise came from. I can tell you his first words or how he looked when he woke up in the morning. My life pretty much stopped when my son was stolen from me, but his life went on. He experienced everything without me. He made memories of his own. He had a whole new life that I wasn't a part of. He called someone else mom and dad. I never imagined that a simple sketch could bring so many painful memories to the surface. Such an innocent face stared back at me, so full of life. Where was my son? Please bring home my son. Silent tears slid down my face. This is how Doug found me when he came home from the hospital. I was still on my knees holding Tim's picture and crying. We decided that maybe it was not such a good idea to hang the portrait yet. Doug carefully wrapped it back up and put it in Tim's closet. Maybe someday he thought but not today. That night he held Faye, they clung to each other. In the morning he put a single red rose on the pillow next to her brushed a sweet kiss across her forehead and slipped away to work. His wife was vulnerable last night, she let him in they shared her thoughts. They somehow found each other through the pain it was beautiful. There was still desire there always had been.

Chapter X

(Could It Be?)

Faye called me here at work, but I was performing a surgery at that time. My nurse said that Faye sounded very agitated and said that it was extremely important that I call home immediately. She even wanted my nurse to get me out of the OR? Now I was worried because nothing out of the ordinary ever happened in our lives anymore. There was never anything pressing and urgent these days except my job. I adored my wife, but I loved coming to work. Here I had a purpose. I did important things. I saved lives every day. As a matter of a fact today I was operating on a young teenage boy who got hurt during football practice. He tore his rotating cuff and damaged his ACL. I imagined that I was seeing Timmy play football and make his first touchdown. It was actually very difficult to concentrate on my surgical procedure. My mind kept wandering. But I'm professional so I finished the procedure and had the nurse suture him up. I cleaned up and thought about calling Faye. I miss the old Faye, she used to get excited and want to hear all about my procedures or even just about my day. Now she was always in her own little world and nothing phased her. So, what could be so pressing? Hmmm? I was very curious...Nothing prepared me for the news I was about to hear...Nothing.

I was going to call Faye but the more I thought about it the more worried I suddenly became. What if they had found Timmy's remains and Faye's carefully constructed world would come crashing down. There was no one home to help her through this. So, I got in my car and begrudgingly drove home quickly. The long ride home was agony and gave me time to think. I loved my wife but there had to be more to life than this. I scolded myself how could I ever think that way? Maybe I should have tried to call her first? What if she was hurt? I'm a terrible person and a worse husband. Sometimes I love being at work more than I love being home. Even amidst the chaos it's normal there. There are no guilty feelings. There are no excuses either...You either save someone and heal them or you don't. Being a surgical doctor is easier than being a husband. I don't consider myself a father anymore because let's face it all my children are dead...All of them. Anyway, when I pulled up in the driveway, I was relieved to see that there were no police there. I burst through the door expecting something terrible.

Faye was in the living room sitting on the couch hugging her arms to her stomach and sobbing. "What is it honey? Are you hurt?" She looked up at me and through her tears she smiled and said..." Doug were going to have a baby. I have a feeling deep down in my bones that this time Doug, this time everything is going to be fine!" She then explained to me that she had known for a while and there had been no warning signs. She always wore big shirts and sweatpants so I had no idea how far along she was. "She hadn't seen a doctor; I know this because she never left the house. How could she have known that everything was fine?" Hell, I'm a doctor and she never told even me. I deduced that since she never left the house, I am very sure she never got examined. As many complications as she has had in her past pregnancies how could she take the chance? I was becoming extremely angry at Faye's irresponsibility and just as I started to open my mouth and speak the harsh words that were swimming around in my head I stopped and finally looked at her, really looked at her and saw the joy in her eyes. It's then that I noticed the subtle changes in her. Her face was a little puffy but there was a glow about her. How could I have not noticed these things? I saw her every day. Then I felt horrible, I was so wrapped up in surviving and holding my breath for the next catastrophe I forgot that life does go on. Faye found a way to cope so maybe it's time for me to actually hope again. Maybe I was allowed my "happily-ever-after?" Just maybe...That night was the first time in a long time there was actually joy in my heart. It felt wonderful to fall asleep with my beautiful wife in my arms. For once we didn't go to bed thinking of Timmy or Catherine or anyone...just us and the last chance at happiness that now grew in Faye's belly. We dreamt of salvation. This baby was our last chance at happiness...He or she had big shoes to fill. Was it fair to lay so much on such tiny shoulders? What would happen if this baby did not survive? Would we? Would Faye? Once again, I found myself holding my breath. Hoping for the best but expecting the worst. That was after all the story of our lives. Sleep was long in coming that night, the new worries had begun. But I never let on...Faye's happiness was contagious, and I basked in it. There was happiness and laughter in our home again and it felt good, I never wanted this feeling to end. We slept in each other's arms. We laughed through breakfast, we made plans for the future. Faye was not worried, I kept it hidden but I worried for the both of us. Nothing bothered her right now and that was beautiful.

Chapter XI

(The pregnancy)

Faye awoke bright and early the next day and she was very busy writing things down when I finally awoke. "Whatcha doing, I asked?" Faye gave me that knowing look and proceeded to tell me exactly how it was going to be..." First of all, we need to move our bedroom downstairs. I don't want to go up and down the stairs at all if I can help it and not unless I absolutely have to." I agreed with her, we we're going to take every precaution there was to keep her safe. "Secondly, the Grocer will have to come here twice per week now. I will have a list of fresh fruits and vegetables I want and will eat on a daily basis. I need to eat fresh fruits and vegetables at least three times per day...I also don't want them sprayed with any type of chemicals." "Oh, and honey...I need lots of catalogs so I can list and circle everything I need you to pick up." She then smiled (something that I hadn't seen in so long it touched my heart.), she said..." Doug, this time I know in my heart of hearts that everything is going to be just fine." On that note I happily kissed my wife and skipped out the door to accomplish all the tasks my wife had lovingly set before me. While in the car I thought to myself, for once I am glad that my wife never left the house because there, I could keep her safe. There were no outside influences that could harm her in the safe haven of our home. This baby was our last chance, I knew it and Faye refused to have any negative thoughts. I knew I'd worry enough for the both of us. If we ever hoped for any normalcy in our life at all, everything rested on some very tiny unborn child that Faye was carrying. Such a large burden for such a small being. I made a promise to myself that no matter what, Faye and our child were going to be alright, my god they had to be. So much tragedy has befallen us and deep down I knew that this was it, this was our very last chance.

I quickly and efficiently completed every task on my honey-do list. I found a doctor that agreed to come to the house. I filled her in on all the complications we had experienced. At first, she questioned why Faye would not go to the hospital. After much explaining she finally understood. When she met Faye it all became crystal clear as well. Just as a back-up I also found a mid-wife that agreed to be a part of this birth as well. She lived close and this way I knew if Dr. Collins was in surgery or unavailable Annabelle would be there in a hot minute. I even suggested that Annabelle move into the house but both Faye and Annabelle declined this idea. Annabelle lives very close, so my begging and pleading fell on deaf ears. Every day when I came home, I found Faye happily circling items that she wanted in her catalogs and there I went again...But I didn't mind. Off to all the stores to purchase her heart's desire. Pretty soon our home was filled with baby stuff. It all stayed downstairs because the nursery was upstairs. My weekends were filled with painting and putting baby furniture together. I transformed an empty room into a beautiful little piece of heaven for our baby. Faye was pregnant throughout the holidays. This year we had a wonderful Christmas...Just the two us and her growing belly. Christmas morning our baby kicked for the first time. The day went beautifully no sadness and if Timmy was on her mind for once he wasn't mentioned. This was a change because the normal Christmas for us always started out joyous and ended in Faye getting that sorrowful look in her eyes when only Timmy's gifts were left...she would lock herself in her room and cry for hours until she fell into a fitful sleep. I would finally get her to unlock the door at which time I would always sit by the bed and stroke her hair and wipe her tears away. In her sleep she would call out to Timmy. I never looked forward to Christmas and Timmy's birthdays was worse. Can you imagine for one minute what it is like having a birthday party for a dead boy? Cake and ice cream, no friends because he has none. Opening his presents because he is not there to do it. And watching Faye's happiness turn to sadness. That was our life until this Christmas. This Christmas we had a lovely dinner and laughed and sang carols. Later in the evening as I held Faye, we discussed baby names. I finally felt some peace wash over me...And another foreign feeling, I felt hope and it felt good. Dr. Collins came often now, she assured me that everything was as it should be. No complications this time just a normal high-risk pregnancy. No Pre-Eclampsia, Faye had not even experienced any morning sickness (at least none that she told me about.) The baby was kicking a lot now, and Dr. Collins said we would be having a heathy baby in a few short months. I was keeping my fingers crossed and I was holding my breath. Not Faye, I hadn't seen her this happy since she was pregnant with Timmy. She didn't have a care in the world. It was almost as if she was floating on cloud nine. She was so peaceful and relaxed. For a little while things seemed almost normal. Because Faye was at home, we never had an ultrasound so this baby would be a surprise. As the end of the pregnancy drew near, I was a little sad. New worries set in now. Hopes and dreams for our future were something I had all but given up on. Here I was hoping again. I even did something that I didn't do very often, I went to the cemetery and talked to mom. "Life has a way of getting in the way, I should come visit more often" ...this is how I began my conversation with Edna, my mother, my best friend. "I'm sorry I haven't been by; I really have no excuse." I told her about my work, I told her that her garden was beautiful and then I shared our news. "I meant to tell you sooner, but we wanted to be sure." After my conversation with mom, I returned to my wife. Timmy's birthday was coming up fast and this was always a hard time for Faye. This time though we were in for a surprise.

Chapter XII

(Cassie)

Faye went into labor the night before Timmy's birthday and gave birth to a beautiful baby girl on Timmy's birthday. We named her Cassie. Cassie was healthy and strong. Her skin was rosy her cheeks were chubby, and I've never seen a baby smile so much in all my life. This little ray of sunshine saved my life and brought that spark back into Faye's eyes. Cassie was such a good baby, she slept through the night quickly and hit every milestone with flying colors. If I could say there was ever a perfect baby it was Cassie. She was a female version of Timmy, blonde curly hair and deep blue eyes and the dimples...My baby was gorgeous she looked just like her momma. Faye was an excellent mother always fussing over Cassie. She used cloth diapers, made her own baby food. Faye was filling the role of a lifetime. This was what she was meant to do, and she relished every moment of it. Cassie grew fast and it was wonderful. Faye wanted to do everything for our baby girl, but Cassie was very inquisitive and independent and wanted to do it all herself. She learned very quickly. Her zeal for life was infectious and her laughter was contagious. I found myself counting the minutes during the workday until I could rush home and be with my perfect little family. Laughter filled our hearts and our house became a home once again and this little girl was the cause. When Faye was pregnant, and I questioned whether or not such a little being could shoulder such a responsibility on her shoulders God saw fit to provide me with just that warrior. I owed Cassie my life and I know Faye felt the same. We were whole again; we were one and nothing and no one was ever going to destroy this...My little happily ever after.

Faye always told Cassie stories about Timmy and Oma Edna. She would talk about them for hours. Cassie listened intently as if she knew in her small toddler head that although these people really meant nothing to her they were extremely important to her mother. As soon as she started walking and talking Cassie could tell you all about Timmy. His favorite foods, colors...what he liked to do. So, although she never met him, she knew he was her older brother and she knew like her parents she loved him. Even when her mother told her that someday she would meet her big brother, it was all very confusing for such a little mind to grasp. But Cassie listened intently because it meant that she had her mother's undivided attention and she loved it. Maybe Cassie would meet him someday and then again maybe not. She loved him either way because he was her brother. She still wasn't quite sure where he was and why he wasn't here? If he was loved so much he should be here. You see, because Faye never left the house she had a phobia for Cassie to leave also. The bond between mother and daughter was extraordinary. They did everything together. They baked and cooked and read stories. We had a room of nothing but games Cassie's favorite game was Operation...go figure, her father was a doctor. Sometimes though Cassie would stand at the window on her tippy-toes and look longingly outside, it was at those times I knew that she wouldn't stay house-bound for long. How would Faye cope? Time would tell...

Late at night when I could pry Cassie away from Faye and put our sleeping child to bed, I would try and talk to Faye. I explained to her that it was unhealthy to keep such an inquisitive child cooped up in the house all day. She needed to explore, skin her knees, and be a normal kid...I didn't want her to fear the unknown and right now that's what the outside was, it was the unknown. I told Faye that Cassie had to someday live in that world, and we weren't doing her any favors by keeping her in a protected bubble. I tried to make Faye understand that someday Cassie would have to go to school. I knew my wife was very capable of home-schooling Cassie, but I wanted her to interact and develop relationships with other kids. This is something she could not do in our house. As I was explaining this to Faye I happened to look up and I saw the panicked look in her eyes. This happened every time I brought these subjects up. She was so afraid to let Cassie out of her sight and her phobia of going outside had gotten worse since Cassie had come into our lives. I guess telling Faye that by preventing Cassie from going outside would cause her to resent her mother wasn't the smartest thing to say. I just worried, I wanted Cassie to be a normal girl with friends and school and everyday functions. This is the only subject we ever argued about. I knew eventually this is one argument I would win. But for today I put it aside and let Faye's bubble stay intact for just a little while longer. I knew that deep down Faye agreed that I was right. She wanted our child to be a normal little girl and not miss out on anything...Everything would work out; I knew this now Faye needed to believe it. Cassie was not yet school aged and when Faye saw how much fun Cassie and I have outside she would eventually do it on her own...Faye is the strongest woman I have ever known, she just needed to believe in herself. She'd get there I had no doubt about it. In time I prayed everything would work out. Maybe, just maybe we could be a normal family. I could only hope.

Faye watched wistfully out the window...Cassie and Doug look so happy out there, not a care in the world. I looked around the room and it seemed to grow smaller. Doug took Cassie outside for a little while each day. She loved it, it is one of the first things she wants to do when Doug got home from work. Am I hurting my daughter? Am I depriving her? This just seems to be the one thing I cannot share with her...Outside. It scares me, I always think to myself, "what if Cassie got hurt? Would I be able to breach the threshold and do what needs to be done?" In that instance I think I'd put my fears aside and do what had to be done...I would...wouldn't I? As I watched them play, I so wanted to join them but I couldn't. Right then though it hit me like a ton of bricks. If I showed fear, then eventually Cassie would also have the same fear. I had to re-learn to go outside. If I didn't I would eventually lose my daughter because she would outgrow me. It actually dawned on me how much of her life I would miss. Sadly, now as I looked around my home. It seemed more like a prison now but one of my own making. I created the prison and I'm the only one that could break free of it. I shuddered when I thought of the daunting task ahead. My self-made jail would eventually cause me to lose my family. Cassie would resent me, not now but eventually. Or worse she'd be ashamed of me. I couldn't allow that. I loved my Cassie and I wanted her to love me. Then and there I decided that I would overcome my fear and go outside. This would be my delicious secret until I was ready to share it. This will probably be one of the hardest things I've ever done...But it was time. Doug and Cassie will be so proud of me. They will be so happy, we all will. I have to work extremely hard on this...step one to the rest of my life. I decided the very next day is when I would begin.

Every day when she put her darling daughter down for her noontime nap , Faye began her reprogramming. It was an arduous journey of joining the living again. It was a lot harder than she thought it would be. At first, she thought she could just open the door and walk out. She tried and a wave of nausea hit her and she went to her knees. New plan of attack. She just sat close to the door, there had been an imaginary wall that she did not know until now existed. Faye hadn't realized how bad the phobia was until she tried to open the door and her hands shook uncontrollably, sweat dripped down her brow and she just couldn't do it...Where did this come from. Ok, Faye thought don't get frustrated...I can do this and I will.

First, she was only able to stand about four feet from the door. This went on for a few months. When she was able to do this like it was second nature to her, she ventured a little closer. In her mind the fear was real; sleep was difficult and fitful. Doug noticed but just thought she had a lot on her mind...the anniversary of Timmy's first day of school was drawing ever closer. He didn't say anything because if that wasn't what was bothering her then he didn't want to remind her of it.

Faye started to make progress, she was able to now take a chair and sit in front of the door or window, she still panicked at first but eventually she would sit quietly and read a magazine or listen to soft music (anything to keep her mind off all the awful things she conjured were outside.) Now as soon as Doug and Cassie left to go to the park Faye made a game of opening all the windows, hearing the wind blow and the bird singing...smelling the tea roses Timmy and Edna planted right outside the window. These sounds and smells brought back a flood of memories. All these little things seemed to help. She was even able to move away from the protective wall...baby steps, you have to learn to crawl before you can walk right? Now when her mind conjured up all the terrible creatures that lived outside, she would simply close her eyes and picture grandmother and grandson planting all the roses and when the smell of them wafted in her fears subsided. She had replaced her fears with happy memories. Her first goal had been met. She was exhausted now by the time bedtime came around most nights, sleep was no longer an issue. As soon as she lay her head on her pillow, she was asleep.

She took a deep breath one day and touched the doorknob; no shaking, that was an amazing feeling. She dared to open the door just a crack. When the familiar feeling of fear and pain returned, she quickly sat in her chair and closed her eyes rocking back and forth until her breathing returned to normal. With her eyes closed she concentrated on the sweet sounds, she could hear the honeybees and kids playing way in the background. When next she opened her eyes, she was fine again. So, the first phase was complete she could actually open the door...a little more every couple of weeks. It was a slow process and what was normal for most people was a struggle for her. It was hard for her to believe that she had once been one of them...you know a normal person. There was finally light at the end of the tunnel! She finally figured out that there was nothing right outside her door that would or could hurt either her or Cassie. It became easier and easier and after a while she looked forward to hearing the sounds and smelling the familiar scents. It was quite something to realize how sterile her environment had been for so many years. She was beginning her life again. She decided that her next step would be to sit in the doorway of the open door. Since it had taken her months to be able to not have a panic attack while sitting with the door open, she got frustrated when she thought about how long it would take to master this much bolder feat. Within 4 months Faye found she could swing her body in-and-out of the doorway. What a glorious feeling! Faye had a goal, Cassie's birthday was three months away and Faye thought it would be wonderful to be able to walk outside and serve their guests. She never dreamed that it would take her this long, almost a full year to breach the confines of her home. There was a whole world awaiting her out there and she wanted to experience it all.

Every day when Doug came home, he would kiss his wife and tell her about his day. Then he would take his impatient daughter by the hand and walk down the hill to the neighborhood park. Cassie was such a clown and so very friendly and outgoing that she has made a lot of friends. They had play dates that Doug set up and Doug took her to. I smiled when I thought to myself that soon it will be me doing these things with my daughter or Doug and I can do it together like a real little family.

Cassie had so many friends now, she wanted all of them at her upcoming birthday party. She and I spent one afternoon doing nothing but making all the invitations for the party, you should have seen us there was glitter and paper and glue everywhere. When Doug got home after we showed him all the invitations, we had made he took Cassie shopping to pick up the decorations for her party, and getting the ingredients not only for a cake but we were going to make homemade ice cream too! Cassie was like a busy bee, everything had to be perfect. Who knew so much went into planning a six-year old's birthday. She wanted a piñata and all kinds of balloons, a bobbing-for-apples barrel and she was very particular about the prizes. This for the girls and that for the boys. She wanted a volleyball net and a tetherball pole. Sack races...She wanted a treasure hunt. This kind of scared me though, you see there were woods behind our house. I made Doug promise me never to take Cassie in the woods. Something about the woods gave me a horrible feeling deep in the pit of my stomach. I couldn't put my finger on it...Just stay away from the woods.

Something was up with Faye, was she excited about our little girl's birthday? Although I knew she wouldn't come outside she was quite content and happy planning it with her daughter. There would never be surprise parties in our house this I promised myself a long time ago. There was a new confidence in her that I hadn't seen in years, it was like looking back in time and seeing the young vivacious gorgeous girl I fell in love with. It was absolutely great. I decided not to question her about it just yet. I was sure that soon we would be facing another bout of major depression. I worried because Faye eats, sleeps and breathes Cassie and when she starts school Faye will be lost. Since she never ventures outside, she will be even more alone and separated from our daughter. So, I will relish Faye's new found independence and deal with the depression when it comes.

Everyday I'm a little braver...now I can actually swing in the porch swing on my deck facing the backyard. Cassie's birthday is a week away I think tonight when Cassie and Doug leave and go to the park, I will greet them on the porch swing with homemade lemonade and chocolate chip cookies! I'm so excited! Well, I guess I better get busy on the cookies...I smile to myself when I think about the shock I'll see in their faces when I come out bearing gifts.

I must admit I am very nervous. The time arrives and Doug and Cassie just returned from the park and are in the yard inspecting their flower garden that they had planted earlier in the year. Here I go, one step at a time. When they come back up the hill I'll be sitting in my swing. Cassie was the first one to spot me. She dropped her dad's hand and ran and jumped into my arms. She was so happy! All she kept saying was, "Mommy, Mommy I knew you could do it! Daddy was right...he said someday you just would. Oh, Mommy I love you!" Then she wrapped her little arms around me and showered me with Cassie kisses. I have never seen her so happy. Now Cassie and I could play outside and set up bird feeders...The world was suddenly a much bigger place, and I was a very happy woman.

I happened to glance over at Doug, he made my heart skip a beat. He had tears streaming down his face. I never realized how much it affected him that I was a recluse. I saw now the pain and guilt I had been causing him all these years. We were healing. When Doug realized that I was watching him, he quickly looked away out of embarrassment and at that moment I fell in love with him all over again. Most couples don't survive what we've been through...with us it just made us stronger. I guess when you lose so much, thinking about losing each other was unfathomable. Doug had stolen my heart years ago...but how can you steal what has always been readily given freely? While I was lost in memories and thoughts it was that moment that Doug startled me by grabbing both Cassie and I in a huge bear hug.

There she was...outside! "Oh Faye, I'm so proud of you.," Doug said as the tears flowed freely down his face. I pulled them into a big bear hug. I was so proud of her. I couldn't believe it...I never thought seeing someone outside could make me so happy. What people take for granted everyday my Faye had I'm sure struggled to do. I was in awe of the woman that stood before me, her strength and courage were something to behold. At that moment Doug said something he thought he'd never dreamed possible..." How would you girls like to have a picnic outside tonight?" Both Cassie and

Faye both readily agreed. Cassie and I decided to run to the grocery store and get the supplies. Faye disappeared into the kitchen to throw some salad and drinks etc. together. For the first time in a long time, they actually seemed like a normal family. When Cassie and Doug got back Faye was in the kitchen slicing and dicing. Cassie put the groceries away and Doug lit the grill. Cassie talked and talked...Faye smiled and thought about how almost perfect this was. Perfection would have been her strapping son outside helping his dad light the grill and playing basketball or talking about sports or cars...Faye quickly snapped out of it as Cassie grabbed her skirt and looked up at her questioningly? "What's wrong Mommy? You looked so far away? But as Cassie asked, she already knew the answer...Timmy. She had never met him but she knew him. She knew he was taken and that's why mommy never went outside. She knew he was taken on her birthday eight years ago. He would be sixteen now. She was turning six. She knew that mommy never gave up hope and that someday Cassie would see him. She was not sure how or when but she knew she'd see her brother. That was both a warm yet very unsettling feeling. Cassie would always talk to Doug about him but never Faye. She made a mental note to ask why she was so apprehensive about meeting Timmy. Dad would know, he knew everything. Doug was the smartest person she knew.

Chapter XIII

(The Picnic)

They all pitched in to create the best picnic they had ever had. There was potato salad and watermelon, fried chicken and hamburgers, hotdogs and sausages. You would think they were feeding an army but no...just the three of them. Cassie tossed the salad and added the ingredients just as soon as Faye had them cut up. There were fresh lemons in the lemonade and a giant fruit bowl. All of Cassie's favorite foods, especially the fruit bowl...Cassie's all-time favorite! Faye put fresh pineapple, peaches, strawberries, apples and grapes. Orange wedges and melons...the list went on and on. This was going to be the best dinner ever; they were all together enjoying the wonderful outdoors as a family. After dinner Faye brought out the fresh homemade chocolate chip cookies she had made. I don't think any of us had ever eaten and laughed so much. I will never take the simple things in life for granted ever again...Those are the best times by far. Making memories for the ones you love and with the ones you love are all you need in life to be happy.

I watched Faye and Cassie run from one end of the yard to the other. There was a full moon and a lot of stars out so there was lots of light. The soft glow from the ebbing fire added to the ambiance. They were laughing and when Faye wasn't swinging Cassie in the air they were chasing and catching fireflies. It's as if they were rediscovering each other and it was a beautiful sight. Rolling in the grass down the hill and pulling the petals off the four leaf clovers and making wishes. Cassie's wishes were that this night would never end...Faye wished that too, but I knew Faye and I knew he was never far from her mind and her heart...Timmy.

I had such a wonderful time with Cassie. We played and chased each other. She let me swing her..." I want to touch the stars' mommy...swing me higher!" She shouted with glee. She was already making plans for the next day...A tea party by the garden...Could we go down the hill to the playground? I just smiled and swung her higher. So much happiness but pain as well. Where was my son? Did someone play with him? Did he touch the stars and have big dreams of hunting wild game while exploring his yard? Did he play football? What was his girlfriend like? Did he ever think of me? Did he blame me? So many thoughts running through my head...But back to realty...I had a little girl that wanted to catch lightening bugs! We caught so many lightening bugs and once again Doug calmly explained to a very inquisitive child why they lit up. "No, Cassie we can't keep them as pets." We made lightening bug lanterns and promised Cassie that they would be there again the next time she wanted to make lanterns. This felt like heaven, I was watching my beautiful wife and daughter discovering each other all over again. This was a magical time for all of us. I thought about how miserable we were before Cassie came along. The weak frail woman of yesteryear was no more. Before me was a beautiful and very strong woman that had overcome so many obstacles, it was still a miracle that she was even here. I thanked God everyday though because if I didn't have my Faye...life would just not be worth living for me. I love her more today than I did yesterday. I loved her on our wedding day but now my deep feelings of pride and admiration and oh so much love were overflowing. Some men think it's hard to give themselves only to one woman. But through the years Faye has matured and the young girl I loved and married has turned into not only a mother but a friend and a lover that I think sometimes knows me better than I know myself. If your partner can not only be your lover but your confidant, your cohort in crime and your best friend then you have the best of both worlds. If you are just as happy to see them as they are to see you at the end of the day, then never let go. As I pondered these thoughts, I wasn't aware that Cassie came up just then and she whispered in my ear..." Daddy wishes do come true, Mommy is outside playing with me!" She gave me a big sloppy Cassie kiss, a quick hug and then she was off to show her Mommy all the flowers we planted. I had never seen them so happy. They were walking hand-in-hand planning another beautiful flower garden complete with a koi pond. They were acting like two little school girls. That really struck me as an odd comparison because one hadn't started school yet and the other had been out of school for quite a few years.

As our evening drew to a close, we tossed all the fruit and salad and corn in the yard for the squirrels and the forest animals. They always came out when we went to bed. With Cassie on my shoulders and Faye's hand in mine we retired into the house to clean up our mess and put our tired girl to bed. While Cassie was upstairs washing the outside off, I turned towards Faye...cupped her face in my hands and asked her, "How did all this happened? When did you do this?" As she regaled the entire story to me, I told her that I was never so proud of anyone in all my life. She told me she still had a long way to go, she still became paralyzed with fear when she thought about getting into the car again and driving was completely out of the question. I laughed and told her that we were better off with me driving because she had no sense of direction. Lord only knows where we'd end up! We both laughed at that as she gently shoved me away. But then she told me that when she thought about leaving the confines of their property she felt as if she were going to panic. I just smiled and told her that she had accomplished so much more on her own than most people could or would in therapy with years of sessions. "Faye, I have every faith in your ability, just take it slow as you need to lean on me, that's what I'm here for. You don't have to do everything alone Silly Ducky! I love you and I will do everything within my power to help you." Faye held me this time not as a scared and helpless woman, she was not unsure or needy...she held me as my equal. That was an absolutely wonderful feeling. Cassie's birthday was in two days and for once I was looking forward to an event. Even though Cassie and Timmy shared the same birthday. But for some reason...try as I might, I couldn't get rid of the little tickle that told me even with all the happiness we were experiencing, "Don't let your guard down." My sixth sense was tingling...I shrugged it off, what could possibly go wrong? I slept fitfully that night, but I slept.

Chapter XIV

(the Birthday Party)

I actually woke up refreshed, there was so much to do today. After a giant breakfast of pancakes and eggs...the feeling of dread was gone if just for a little while. Faye had quite the grocery list for Cassie and I and off we went! Party favors, food, drinks, games...We had to make sure that everything was perfect...You only turn six once! As for Cassie's cake, she wanted a cake in the shape of a teddy bear in a pink poncho with a pink flower behind her ear. With so many years of being cooped up in the house Faye had become an expert baker and quite the chef. She insisted on making Cassie's cake. After baking and decorating Cassie's cake Faye added her very own special touch. She purchased a locket to put around the bears wrist. While it was beautiful it served a purpose. On the inside were pictures, the left side had a picture of Faye and myself and the right side had a picture of Cassie. On the back was Cassie's phone number and address. Faye figured she couldn't protect her all the time and in her mind, I knew that now she reasoned if Cassie ever got lost she'd never forget where home was. This was her way of letting our little girl venture out into the big bad world with her blessing...even if her big bad world so far consisted of the park and kindergarten and trips to town with dad. She had the bracelet special ordered to match the bear...white gold because it is stronger and outlined in pink to match the bear. Cassie didn't know about the bracelet and I had stumbled onto it by surprise. Fay was the most thoughtful person I knew. She always put everyone else's needs in front of her own. Cassie will see the beautiful bracelet and love it because of the thought and care that went into it...I knew the hidden meaning behind it.

After a few tedious hours and quite a few choice words her cake was complete with the bracelet strategically placed in plain sight around the bear's wrist. "Quite the masterpiece I'm quite proud of myself," Faye thought. She smiled at her creation let's see how well Cassie pays attention to detail. With that the teddy went into the refrigerator. The rest of the day was spent cooking and preparing everything for the party. That evening we all retired early because planning a six-year-olds birthday party is extremely exhausting. Besides, we would have to get up pretty early so we could set everything up. People were going to start showing up around 1pm in the afternoon. We wanted to be able to have a little family time for ourselves before we had to share our precious little girl with everyone else. We had some special gifts for her and Faye had to have her time to celebrate Timmy. I knew this and even though I loved my son dearly, he was gone. Faye had a ritual, first she would light a candle and put it in his room. Sit on his bed and hold his pillow. She would cry and hug that pillow as if sending all her love through it to our son. Faye also made him a cake every year and decorated his room. She needed this private time and Cassie and I learned to just let her go through it. I knew Timmy was gone. Cassie even deduced on her own that he was gone...Faye steadfastly believed that he would return. I think deep down she knew but to let go was to admit it and she couldn't imagine anything bad ever happening to him. She had made herself believe that the "people" that took him had the best intentions in mind. Honestly though, if you snatch a child, it's never for the good. Bad people do bad things. In my book I believe that people aren't born bad and you can only blame mom or dad for so long...eventually people grow up and make choices. Whomever took my son had bad intentions and I know this sounds cruel but I hope he died quickly and painlessly. I hope he wasn't scared...I try not to think about it anymore the guilt is almost unbearable. But yes the guilt is still there. And today as Faye softly cries in his bedroom I wrestle with my own demons about that fateful day. "I'm so sorry my son...I have failed you in the worst way possible, I didn't protect you. Please forgive me." I hang my head and slowly walk away from the muffled sobs coming from behind Timmy's locked door. I made a vow that nothing and no one will ever harm a hair on Cassie's head...I will protect her with my dying breath. Woes the person that makes her cry. Will anyone ever be good enough for her...hmmm, that remains to be seen.

I had to shake it off and knowing Faye, after her cry she'll shower and come downstairs looking like a rose. Behind every smile is a cascade of tears waiting to fall...but this is Cassie's day and we want her to remember it with love and laughter and good times had by all. Mask the pain, quell the fear...but that feeling of dread is back stronger than ever. No time for that now, I had the outside to decorate. We had Piñatas to set up and games to hang and prepare. I had to hide all the clues for the treasure hunt, the Pin-the-tail-on-the-donkey needed to be hung. Water in the apple barrel. I finished it all with time to light the grill for the burgers and dogs! Cassie and I helped Faye set up all the food and beverages. It was a lot of hard work making a six-year-olds birthday the absolute best it can be. I actually couldn't wait to be done with the busy work and plant myself behind the grill where I could relax, drink a beer and enjoy the festivities. It dawned on me then that if Faye hadn't made herself come outside...this would have all been on me. Wow, thank you Faye...I definitely could not have done this! Cassie was at the point of bouncing off the walls! It was so good to see my little daughter and wife so excited. Looking at Faye now and seeing her smile is a far cry from the woman that was upstairs not only three hours ago in so much pain and agony. I looked at Faye and felt I should pinch myself because this felt almost normal. Could we finally live happily-ever-after? I hope so...God I pray so.

The doorbell rings, yep it's 1pm and here come all the kids and the parents. It's kind of funny all of Cassie's friends and their parents know me and of course Cassie but none of them had ever seen Faye. I'm sure some of them if not most of them thought that I was raising Cassie alone. They never asked, but I had heard the whispers and seen the sad looks.... Is he divorced? Is he a widower? Poor Doug, raising that baby all alone. It was quite comical. Many of the moms had put the moves on Doug. Maybe they thought he was gay? Would they be in for a surprise! The ones that actually took the time to ask were expecting a quiet, very shy and reclusive woman...You should have seen their faces when they met my beautiful, bubbly and very happy wife. And Cassie was beaming, poor Faye, Cassie made it her mission to introduce her to every one of her friends and all of their parents. Faye took it like a trooper. Would she remember all the names? This is the woman that had not had anyone except myself and Cassie for all of these years. She had no friends...well until this afternoon anyway! Now she had lunches and teas and promised playdates. I almost felt jealous, I was used to having her all to myself and now all of a sudden, I had to share...Quite a different feeling I must say. A smiled played across my lips though...because now we were a quote-un-quote normal family.

Let the party begin! The nagging feeling had subsided and the look on Cassie's face was worth more to me than all the gold in the world. Doug looked like the cat that swallowed the canary. It was such a beautiful day. Not too hot and not too cold. The sun was shining and the kids were playing. Doug was finally relaxing...I guess I never realized how tense he had been. I was getting used to the deep belly laughs again and it was wonderful. Music to my ears if you will; then there were Cassie's little snickers she had such a cute laugh...I had never really noticed. And the amount of friends she has, I have missed out on so much...No more! Life was for the living and I wanted to live. I just can't help wishing that Timmy were here. After-all today was his birthday too. He is sixteen years old today. I could feel the familiar sadness creeping ever so slightly in...Not today, not in front of Doug or Cassie...I could cry later in the shower when I would be alone. They have been through so much, enjoy today my loves, enjoy today.

Chapter XV

(Cassie's day)

So many friends, I don't know who to play with first...Oh well, maybe we can all play a game together? Hmmm.... "Dad – Daddy, can we do the treasure hunt?" I'm so excited...mommy made up the clues so that everything would be fair but I got to pick out the different colors. The clues were different colors and covered in glitter. Daddy said the magic words..." Treasure hunt it is, yay!!!" Everyone has a treasure map. There are seven clues. "Ok, I'll read clue one" dad said and then you are all on your own! Clue one, "If you are in a hungry mood, go here first and take some food." Everyone ran towards the house but me. I know mom and she likes to keep her house clean so I'm guessing the food is where dad is...The grill! Yes! I'm right! Clue number two: "You're probably thinking what the heck! You might want to check out the deck." Everyone is still searching for the first clue and I'm already on the third one! How exciting!!!Time for number three..." When it's extremely cold you can't leave me out. Everyone needs me for their garden to sprout." Wow that one is tough, except that daddy and I plant a garden every year...What is it that we use? I know-I know, the hose!!!We use it all summer and have to put it away in the winter so that it doesn't crack because of the cold! I found the next clue! Looks to me like all the others are still only on clue number two! Ok, here I go number four! "During the warm weather you stand, kneel, work and sweat in me. I like the sun and the rain but I can't be in the shade of a tree." I happened to glance over at the garden daddy and I planted and I think...yep I do see a small blue piece of paper! Clue number five, "Don't be sappy! Stay rooted by branching out on this object." Hmmm...that sounds like daddy's trees by the edge of our yard?" I'm never allowed to go by the trees but this is a treasure hunt. Not everyone is playing some of the boys are playing kickball...oh no, there goes the ball past the trees. I can get it..." Hold on!" Oh wow, it's pretty in here...look at the honeybees and the butterflies! (Cassie walks farther into the woods.) Pretty soon she can hardly hear the others...to busy looking around. "Why am I not allowed to come out here it's so cool!!!" Pretty soon Cassie forgot why she even came into the woods...she forgot all about the boys and the ball.

No one noticed her missing for quite a while. There were so many kids and Doug was busy cooking burgers and dogs. Faye on the other hand try as she might was being pulled here and there. So many mothers wanting to know how she could bear to stay in the house for so long. They asked a lot of questions that she wasn't ready to answer yet. Some whispered and smiled to her face...I guess people judge what they don't understand. Faye just smiled and made small talk.

It had been a while since she had espied her daughter anywhere and she was starting to get concerned. She made her way over to Doug and soon they were both looking for her. Meanwhile...

Chapter XVI

(the fall)

There's a crash that's followed by a loud thud then nothing. An eerie silence as Cassie falls into complete darkness...She lays motionless. Drifting in and out of consciousness "W-where am I? It's cold down here and I hurt.... Mommy...I want my mommy...Daddy, daddy...I want my daddy." (Cassie cries unheard by those searching for her.) Soon she falls asleep again, it's very cold in this dark place.

She was just here? Where is she? Oh my god...not again, please not again! "Doug where is Cassie?" I've got to find my daughter! "Please someone help me! Where's Cassie?" Doug is checking the house...Everyone is looking for her...She has vanished; she's gone just like my Timmy. Oh God...there's Doug..." Doug, Doug did you find her?" All the color has drained from his face...She's not in the house?" I went down to my knees...sobbing uncontrollably begging someone to find my baby." Then I looked towards the woods and dread filled every fiber of my being. Please no, she went to the woods. "Doug she went to the woods!"

Oh please not again...Cassie? "Where's Faye? I ran over to her she is on her knees...Get up we have to find Cassie!! Then it's back...the feeling I've been trying to lose all day and I looked towards the trees. Maybe she's just lost? I sprint towards the woods; I have to find Cassie. I looked back and everyone is following my lead now...Cassie we start yelling. Not a sound, the woods are quiet...I don't hear anything except the blood pumping through my own veins and my heartbeat. I feel fear, she has to be here...Cassie I yell. Silence, nothing but dead silence. Everyone instinctively lined up and started calling her name but there is nothing. After a while, what seemed like hours the parents start to give up the search. They have to get their own children home. Someone called the police, they are trying to get me to leave the woods. I can't, somewhere in those dark woods my daughter is helpless and afraid...She may be hurt. I'm not leaving without my Cassie. Where is Faye? Oh God...Faye. I haven't thought about her since all this happened. We have been so careful; I should have put up a fence years ago. I should have cut back the over-growth, I didn't. We instilled in Cassie never to go near the woods...Why did she do it? Where is she? There are flashlights now and search dogs...Officer Jess is here. He's trying to sooth Faye. I can hear the things he's telling her, "If she's out here the dogs will find her, I promise you.". The parents are whispering amongst themselves...They recognize us now; they think it odd that now two of our children have just disappeared. I don't care what they think...just find my daughter.

Cassie woke up and thought she was having a bad dream. Her arm was hurting and she couldn't move her legs. She was cold and scared and didn't know where she was. Last she remembered she was at her birthday party having a treasure hunt. The woods...she's in the woods but where? Her eyes had gotten used to her surroundings so she was able to make out something leaning against the wall. What was it? As hard as she tried to move closer to it, her legs didn't want to work. It was also very cold down here "wherever here was?" It smelled funny here and she realized she was sitting in water? When she looked up she could no longer see the light out of a very small hole. Maybe it was night time? All she knew is that she was cold and tired and very very afraid. Where was mommy and daddy? Why hadn't they found her yet? When she opened her mouth to yell nothing more than a hoarse whisper emerged. She hadn't had anything to drink for a while and she definitely wasn't going to drink this nasty water it smelled funny. She looked around and realized she was in a well. But this well had not been used in a long time by the looks of it. In the corner she saw what looked like a backpack and a teddy bear? Those were really strange things to find in an abandoned well? She couldn't make out what the lump was leaning against the wall? Almost looked like a small person. Why would there be a person in the well and why wasn't the person trying to help her? "Hey, hey you...can you help me find my mom and my dad? I'm scared and I want to go home...Hey, how come you won't talk to me? Is that your bear and backpack?" Maybe he or she is asleep...Cassie thought. She used her arms drug and clawed her way to the side of the well that is closest to her. That really hurt, thank goodness daddy is a doctor he can fix me...But first he has to find me. She leaned her head against the wall and snatched the old dirty teddy bear out of the smelly water, hugged it close to her and drifted off into a cold fitful sleep.

It was happening again...dogs and police, search parties. I-I can't do this again. Where was my Cassie? Her birthday was so perfect until it wasn't. "Take this the doctor said, try to sleep...No-no-no, how can I sleep while my baby is not safely tucked away in her princess room?" Why did they stop searching? Something about it being too dangerous at night in the woods? Yet my daughter was in the woods. She's alone, she's scared...God forbid she may be hurt. And where is Doug? Why isn't he looking for her? Now it's late and it's quiet and starting to rain. Tears silently slid down my cheek...oh please god, please not again I sobbed.

It's raining and I have failed, my baby is lost in the woods. Be brave daddy's girl, do whatever you have to I will find you. I will bring you home. I'm sitting on the windowsill and in the back of my mind I can hear Faye's muffled sobs. As I stare out into the dark and watch the rain slide down the window. I think I'm crying but I'm not sure. I'm numb again, in one split second all my joy was once again wrenched away from me. Cassie has to be alright...I can't believe otherwise, I refuse to. But there is a nagging question that keeps rolling around in my mind and threatens to emerge. If she is ok, then why didn't she cry out when we were searching for her? She could not have gotten that far. Where is my Cassie? I'm so sorry Faye, it was my job to keep you and our daughter safe. I'm a failure yet again. First Timmy and now Cassie. No...Not Cassie, I won't allow it! I don't care what "Officer Friendly" said I'm going searching for my daughter. It's cold, dark and raining and my little girl needs me. "Hold on Cassie, daddy is coming...I willed her to hear me." With that I got the flashlight, put on my rain slicker and slipped out the back door headed into the ominous woods. I had nothing on my mind but finding my little girl. I looked up into the sky as the rain drops stung my eyes and vowed that if there was a god he would help me find my little girl.

D-daddy is that you daddy? I hear daddy!!! "Hey you, daddy will help us both get out of here! I'm sure your mommy and daddy are looking for you too!" I yelled at the top of my lungs..." Daddy I'm here!" I wanted to tell him there was someone down here with me but he'd see soon enough. I was so sore and tired and very cold. I don't know how long I had been down here, thank goodness for this other kid down here with me. He or she doesn't talk much it would have been much scarier to be down here alone. Even though the teddy smelled funny and was wet he reminded me of my bunny on my bed. Cassie thought to herself..." daddy has to hear me" ...more determined than ever she started yelling as loud as she could. Why doesn't this other kid yell? He or she can't be asleep...maybe they don't want to go home? But I do! "DADDY!!!!!" He's getting closer I can hear him...find me please! Maybe if I try and stand up? (Searing pain shoots through Cassie's legs as she tries to stand) Cassie slumps back down in the murky cold water and tears start to trickle down her dirty little face, every move hurt. Disheartened she tried to pull her legs into her body...she was very cold and getting colder.

Where is Cassie? I thought I heard her yell and now nothing. Is my heart willing my mind to hear what it wants? So many thoughts are running through my head. If I can't find her I don't want to live in a world without her. She has been our salvation and now she's gone. God plays evil tricks on people. I'm not going to think the worst, it is late maybe she fell asleep? I'm trying to remember if she at least had a coat on? Why can't I remember? I strain to hear her but all I hear is the beating of my heart and the rustling of the leaves under my shoes. At least it has stopped raining. I hope my little girl is somewhere safe and warm. If I find her...no, I'm not going to think like that. When I find her...damn, I should have brought her a warm coat. I'm just not thinking clear...I have to clear my head and concentrate on every little sound because one of them might be her. "Cassie...Cassie, can you hear me?" I yell...nothing greets me, just dead eerie silence.

The shivering woke Cassie up. It must have been a dream she thinks sadly. She turns to the little person that is in the well with her and asks him if he heard her daddy. She thinks it's a he because of the pants and the "boy tennis shoes." He must be asleep though because he hasn't answered her. She continues to talk to him..." What's your name? Is this your bear? Do you mind if I hold him? Where are your mommy and daddy? How long and why are you down here? Did you fall in like I did? Cassie gets frustrated because she is only answered by silence. But somehow by talking to him Cassie doesn't feel so alone. Her eyes have really adjusted well to the dimly lit area and she sees that the small person in the well with her is a little boy. He is really skinny and all scrunched up in the corner. He is hugging a backpack against his chest. From what she can make out he has blonde hair. She feels a connection to him but she's not sure why. The backpack looks familiar. Hmmm, maybe she saw one like it in the store when she went shopping with daddy? It doesn't matter because when daddy finds her he will also get this little boy out of here and I bet his mommy and daddy will be happy to see him. He seemed really sad to Cassie. He doesn't move or talk...Cassie finally decided that he just sleeps a lot. Cassie starts to nod off again she is really hungry and cold. She slowly starts to scoot over by the little boy hoping maybe he'll keep her warm. Every move she makes is agony but she makes it and leans next to the little boy. She felt some small relief because at least she was not alone anymore.

It's day two, the police are already searching the woods. They started bright and early. I can hear the dogs. I want to help but I can't make myself get out of bed. This is like déjà vu. Every time I close my eyes I see Timmy. I'm numb...when I close my eyes I'm reliving that fateful day that Timmy went missing. Cassie needs me I can't let her down like I did with Timmy. But I can't move, it's as if I'm in a fog. I don't know where Doug went? Was he here this morning? As hard as I try I can't remember. Maybe Cassie is home? With that Faye gets up and runs down the hall and throws open Cassie's door only to be met by the site of a bed that was not slept in, presents that were not opened...Faye slides down the wall outside of Cassie's door and the tears start cascading down her face. She crawls across the room and leans against Cassie's bed. As she runs her hands across the blanket, she feels Bunny and clutches the stuffed rabbit to her chest. Oh my god she realizes that Cassie can't sleep without Bunny. Faye buries her head in the bunny cries herself to sleep...Her haunted dreams are of Timmy and now Cassie they are blended together...It's as if she done this before. A nightmare that she can't wakeup from.

Faye woke with a start; she can't lay here a wallow in self-pity while her daughter needs her. She made the mistake once of giving up and by god it won't happen again. She ran to her room and put on her shoes and long pants and coat. She was determined to find her little girl. She willed Cassie to hear her..." Mommy is coming baby, hang on." She ran to Cassie's room and grabbed Bunny, a warm coat and a blanket for Cassie. She was either going to find her or die trying.

She took the stairs two-at-a-time and barely noticed Doug passed out on the couch. She was on a mission and she would not fail. With a deep breath she threw open the front door and ran out into the cold brisk morning. She sprinted to the woods and passed the threshold that she hadn't dared cross in a very long time. No time to pause or rethink anything...her baby needed her. She walked carefully looking for signs that her daughter had been there. It was hard because of everyone yesterday that had trampled through here. Then she saw it, a wet cold light pink ribbon. She recognized it because she had lovingly placed it around Cassie's ponytail yesterday morning before the party. Cassie had picked that one out special because that was her mommy's favorite color. Renewed hope surged though Faye, she had found a sign. She kept looking and soon about 50 yards away she found one of the treasure hunt clues. Faye found the little blue piece of paper that had clue 5 on it. It was wet and torn and smudged with mud but she knew the clues by heart and each one had been written on a different color of very bright paper. Faye knew on this morning she would find her daughter. Come what may she would find Cassie. The animals had started to stir so now the silent woods were once again teaming with life. Faye called out for Cassie...still nothing. She refused to give up hope, it was as if something or someone was guiding her. She wondered how so many people did not see these clues? There was a clearing up ahead so Faye decided to go there and carefully look. She could not run willy-nilly through the woods she might miss something.

In the clearing she sat down on a mossy green log, the sun was just beginning to peak through the top of the trees. She could feel the warmth on her face, and she smiled because she was not afraid. As a matter-of-a-fact she had not thought of herself at all. She knew that a mother's love for her child was a very powerful weapon and she intended to use all her skill and cunning to track down her wayward lost and probably very scared child. Tonight, Cassie would sleep in her own bed and Faye would watch over her. First thing first, she had to find her. "Cassie, she yelled again...nothing." She was so lost in thought that she almost missed the bright yellow piece of paper...clue number one! Faye had been walking now for over an hour but she wasn't giving up. It would be ironic to find Cassie and then get lost herself. "We'll cross that bridge when we get to it." That's when she saw it...the treasure map. Cassie must be close. "Baby, mommy's here, Cassie can you hear me?"

Cassie was very groggy but she thought she heard her mommy. She asked the little boy if he had heard anything. He didn't answer, he never answered her but he was here and he felt familiar and that comforted her. She leaned closer to him and whispered that they would find his mommy and daddy too. She heard it again louder this time...It is mommy!!! "Mommy, I'm here! Her voice was no more than a whisper and her little body was shaking uncontrollably but she tried again and this time she was a little louder. "Mommy, mommy

I'm here!" She hugged the ravaged little teddy bear to her...Cassie knew she was going home!

That time Faye heard her! Cassie was alive and coming home. But where was she? Faye was three hours into her search and she couldn't see her anywhere. Her voice sounded a little muffled...think Faye think. Then she saw it, she almost missed it. A well, hmmm there was an abandoned well all the way out here in the woods. "Cassie?" She heard the sweetest sound, she heard her baby calling to her. She found Cassie, she was in the well. Fear crept into Faye's mind, was Cassie hurt? How did she get down the well? She looked around inspecting the well, over-grown moss and weeds had hidden it from everyone for so long. The wood on top of it was jagged and splintered. Cassie had most likely tripped and fallen down into the well. No matter, Faye started removing the fallen branches and looked around for a way to get into the well without getting stuck herself. She peered down into the hole but it was pretty deep and dark so she couldn't make out much. "Hold on Cassie, mommy is here and I'm going to get you out ok." It sounded to Faye like Cassie was talking to someone? Something about "we are almost saved and going home?" Faye felt a shiver go up and down her spine. But her mission now was to free her daughter from the well. She looked around and found some branches, she put them down the well and proceeded to shimmy down the branches into the deep dark well. She landed in water about up to her ankle and the smell was horrendous. She tried to look around and when her eyes adjusted to the dim light she spied Cassie leaning up against the side of the well under what looked like a little ledge. It was pretty dark in there and it took a bit for her eyes to adjust.

"Mommy! Mommy! You're here, you found me. Can we help this little boy too? He has been down here a long time. He doesn't talk much but he has helped me. He let me hold on to his teddy bear all night so I wouldn't be scared. We can't leave him down here." Faye looked at the little boy and fell to her knees. She recognized his tattered clothes and the shoes she had bought him to wear to school for the first time. She recognized his teddy. Oh my god...she found her little Timmy. She was numb, so many thoughts racing through her head. She couldn't process this it was too much. She crawled over to him. He was just a skeleton at this point but she brushed a tuft of blonde hair out of his face. When she gazed at him through tear filled eyes she did not see a skeleton she saw her little boy. She saw his dimples and his rosy cheeks, his beautiful blue eyes and she could hear his laughter. She thought to herself that the sweetest sound to a mother's ears is the sound of your child's laugh. Cassie was looking at her mommy now and wondering what was going on? Does mommy know this little boy? She is crying and smiling at the same time. Cassie shook her mommy, "can we go home now mommy?" Faye looked at Cassie and calmly said, "Yes baby-girl we are all going home now, you and me and Timmy." Cassie looked at the little boy, the realization hit her that this was her big brother. Why was he still so little she wondered? He wasn't much bigger than she was? It didn't matter she decided, daddy would explain it to her. He always made sense of things that made no sense to her. Faye gathered up her daughter and put the coat on her that she had brought. She then took her coat off and gently cradled her son in the coat. She gathered up all his things and tied both ends of the coat shut. It was time for Timmy to leave this watery little grave and come back to the bosom of his family that loved him. Yes, Faye knew he was gone but her love for him was strong and fierce, and she was not leaving him down here for one more minute. The climb was hard and she slipped a few times. Cassie was injured in the fall so Faye went very slowly. She wore her coat like a backpack for it held very precious cargo. Finally, as they reached the top Faye crawled out. Covered in mud and water Faye carefully laid the coat down and then turned her concentration onto her daughter. Cassie was wet and cold and shivering uncontrollably but more alarming was the way her leg splayed to the side of her body at a very unnatural angle. She had lots of cuts and bruises and they were all angry and red. Infection was setting in, she needed to get her home. Her brave little girl had not once complained. Faye looked around, she would have to create some kind of stretcher so as not to damage Cassie's leg any more than the fall and the trek out of the well had done. She found some long branches there were a lot of fallen trees around the area and she remembered the blanket she had brought for Cassie. She took the shoelaces out of her shoes and ripped small holes in the fleece blanket so that she could secure it to branches and make it sturdy to transport her daughter out of here. With the make-shift stretcher complete she carefully laid Cassie in it and put her coat backpack on and started the slow ordeal of going home. Cassie quickly fell asleep and as Faye gazed down at her daughter, she saw the dark circles and the paleness of her skin. We weren't out of the woods yet I just knew that I needed to get Cassie home where Doug could assess her condition. Amazingly I found my way to the clearing, and I could hear Officer Jess and Doug calling for me. Soon we were all reunited. Doug was so relieved to see me and then he saw Cassie. Worry creased his brow, he didn't say anything but after living with a man for so many years sometimes the silence is worse. Officer Jess looked worried too. Cassie had not woken up but at least the shivering had ceased a little. Officer Jess took off his coat and covered her. We had about another hour and a half to go until we would be clear of the woods. Actually, it would take longer because we had to go slow. We could not chance picking Cassie up because of her injuries so we went over each bump gingerly. Sometimes we could hear Cassie grimace in her sleep. I was worried because once she closed her eyes she never woke back up. Maybe I thought she was just so relieved to be out of the well and felt safe once again...maybe it was worse. All I knew is that I had my family back together. I hadn't had a chance to tell Doug about Timmy. In all the commotion he hadn't even noticed my make-shift backpack. There would be time to tell everything once we knew Cassie was ok. Cassie had to be ok.

After another two hours we were finally at the edge of the woods that led to our property. Cassie was shivering uncontrollably yet her skin was hot to the touch. She was mumbling incoherently and thrashing about on the stretcher. I felt helpless at this point. Maybe I found her too late? No, I refused to give up on her, we had been through too much today and besides Doug was the best doctor I knew. I had faith in his abilities, and he would make her better. We got her in the house and Officer Jess went up and started a warm bath for her. We put Epsom salt in the water to help with the nasty wounds that were very infected at this point. I explained to Jess and Doug that I had found her in an abandoned well that was calf high in stagnant water and yes Timmy. But I hadn't told them about Timmy yet. Slowly they placed a semi-unconscious little girl into a lukewarm bath so as not to throw her beat up bruised little body into anymore shock than it already was. I knelt by the tub and with a warm wash cloth wiped away all the dirt from her face. Then it happened as I knelt there and softly sung to her Cassie opened her eyes and softly smiled at me. I had saved my daughter...peace filled my soul. She reached out her little hand and brushed away the tears that I didn't even know had started to flow. Although not more than a whisper she said, "Mommy it's going to be alright now, please don't cry." We kept Cassie in the warm water until the shivering subsided and she was a bit more alert. I wanted to give the Epsom salt time to soak into the angry wounds and scratches to relieve some of the pain and discomfort that I knew she had to be feeling. I marveled at my little girl, not once in all of this had I heard her complain. When we got her all cleaned up Officer Jess said he had to go let the station know that Cassie had been found and is in "Doctor's care."

Doug cleared off everything from the kitchen table and laid a clean white sheet across the table so that he could examine Cassie. Some of her wounds were superficial but some were not. It was too late to stitch them so we used some of the glue from his medical bag to seal the deeper wounds and covered them in butterfly bandages to protect them. Doug gave her some antibiotic shots to help her body fight the infection from the stagnant water. Her leg was another problem. Apparently when she fell, she landed on a rock which crushed and splintered her hip. Doug looked at me and told me that she would have to have surgery to repair this. He was going to do the surgery himself but it had to be done now. "Faye, you are going to have to sit in the car and hold her extremely still, any type of movement will cause the splintered bone to do more harm. Can you do this? Can you ride in the car?" I had already started bundling up our daughter for the trip to the hospital. Once I was situated in the back of the car Doug laid Cassie in my arms. "Don't be scared mommy" she said. "Daddy is going to make me all better." Such a brave little girl...my heart swelled with love.

Chapter XVII

(Surgery)

We got to the hospital and Cassie was once again asleep. Doug checked her in and a nurse came in her room to take her vitals and put the IV in her arm. Cassie stirred and winced as the needle pierced her delicate skin but she never woke up. I looked down at my little girl in the big hospital bed and realized just how tiny and helpless she looked. I looked at all the bruises and cuts and my heart broke. Then I looked at her angelic face and her pretty blonde curly hair all tousled and messy. I never knew I could love someone so much yet here she was. She is the best parts of me and I'm in awe of her. I realized then that Cassie had saved me in every way a person can save another person. Everything I overcame I did for her. When I looked into her eyes, I saw a wisdom far beyond her six little years. Doug came in the room to collect her for her surgery. He didn't speak, he didn't have to. I had to be strong for all of us. Doug needed my faith and he had to know that I believed in him. I squeezed his hand and looked knowingly into his eyes and then they were gone. There was no one I would rather have perform this delicate surgery on my little girl. I knew she would be fine.

Minutes turned into hours, I sat then I paced then I sat some more. I had a lot of time to think. So much had happened today. While I was reliving the events of the day and lost in my own thoughts Officer Jess happened in. "A penny for your thoughts" he smiled and said. It dawned on me that no one knew about Timmy. A tear slid down my cheek, Jess reached up and brushed it away. "If you hadn't have found her she might not have made it, don't cry the worst of it is over now. Doug will fix her hip and leg and she'll be good as new." I looked at him deep in his eyes and said, "Jess do you know what it's like to lose a child? There was more in that well then just Cassie." A puzzled look came over his face so I continued, "When I got to the bottom of the well I found another that I have been longing to find for a very long time. You see Cassie and Timmy share the same birthday and on this birthday Cassie found her brother. Timmy was at the bottom of that well." More tears freely flowed down my face and when I looked up Jess was crying too. "Is he still in there...the well I mean he asked?" "Oh god no, I brought both he and Cassie up. I couldn't leave him down there a minute longer. When I found Cassie she was leaning against him. Somehow, he gave her comfort and she was clutching his teddy bear. It is bittersweet, even in death he was strong enough to help Cassie. All these years I never gave up and now there is nothing left. My little boy is dead is dead. I collected all his things from his watery grave and put him and them in my coat. I tied both ends of the coat together and brought him home. I haven't told Doug yet, I'm not sure how." Jess held my hands then, I hadn't realized that I was clutching Bunny so hard that my knuckles were white. He simply looked at me and said," you need to tell him just as you told me. You are the strongest woman I know and anything you or Doug or Cassie need I'm here to help." "There's something else I said, do you remember how towards the end of Edna's life she would sit for hours and talk to someone? On her last day I remember she put her hand on the window and looked towards the woods and said that soon she and Timmy would be together again. I was so angry with her, my little boy was not dead. Now I realize that somehow she knew. Do you think that when your time draws near you are closer to the spirit world then the living world? She knew, all those afternoons when she insisted on sitting outside and stared at the woods and held conversations with what we thought was her imaginary friend...she was actually talking to Timmy." Jess looked at me at that moment and said, "Faye, he may have met his death in that well but he was never alone. Take some comfort in that. Edna has been taking care of his spirit all these years. What you found was just the shell. Your little boy is in heaven. When Cassie needed him he was there to help her. His presence alone took away her fear. His teddy bear comforted her. She was not alone at the bottom of that well she had an angel by her side." Those words brought comfort to my sad soul. After that we just sat in silence each lost in our own thoughts.

Cassie is cleaned and prepped. I've done this surgery a hundred times and while it is never easy it has never been so important or meant so much to me as this one does. I will my hands to stop shaking. My little girl is depending on me. One slip and she may never walk again. I can do this; I will do this. I say a silent prayer and ask god to guide my hands. As I open up Cassie's hip it is quite a mess in there. There are bone fragments and torn muscle everywhere. Her hip looks like raw hamburger. Slowly and meticulously, I suction out the bone fragments and sew layer after layer of muscle together. I watch her vitals because you see the longer someone is under anesthesia the more dangerous it becomes. She was so weakened by her ordeal I was hesitant to open her up. If I hadn't though we ran the risk of amputation. Cassie is strong and healthy so I took the risk and now here we are. After the third hour I finally have all the dead bone and fragments removed and now I can see what we have to work with as far as putting her together. Titanium is going to be the answer. She'll have to have another surgery or two when she gets older as Titanium unlike bone and cartilage will not grow as she matures. But at least she'll be able to walk...I hope she will. Titanium has been placed, all the nerves has been reattached and we are using rubber for the ball sockets for her pelvis so that she can bend her leg. Normally my nurse does the sewing up but no one has touched Cassie but me and I am going to finish this. Sixty stitches later and it's off to recovery. She came through the surgery like a champ. Now the recovery begins. I need to go see Faye and let her know that Cassie will be fine.

Doug came bounding out of the operating room with a huge grin on his face. That could only mean one thing...Cassie was fine. Thank god, my little girl was going to be ok. Jess shook Doug's hand and made his exit this was family time and god knows this family needed all the happy moments they could get. Officer Jess had a mission and he had no intentions of waiting too long to fulfill it.

Doug told Faye all about the surgery and how well Cassie did. She is the strongest little person he knew. When he told Faye about all the damage they were both in awe that she had survived it. The shock alone should have killed her. Doug also told Faye that he was never so proud of her. Faye is the one who found her. Faye who just a few months ago could not leave the house. Faye who feared the woods with a passion. "Look at everything you have done for your daughter, I know where she gets her strength from. I love you so much, everything you have gone through and look at you now. This is not the same woman that I married. You are my hero." They held each other and cried tears of relief. After what seemed like an eternity Doug asked Faye if she'd like to go see her daughter. "Cassie should be waking up soon and I know she is going to want her mommy and Miss Bunny." With that said they walked hand in hand to Cassie's room. When they entered the room the nurse was checking Cassie's vitals. "She is doing fine Dr. Peterson; she should be waking up any time now." "Thank you Sandy, I got it from here go on and take a break." I looked at Faye and motioned for her to sit in the chair next to Cassie's bed. I wanted her first memory of waking up to be her mommy. Faye caressed Cassie's small little hand. She would be there for her daughter, help her with whatever she needed. The recovery that Cassie faced was not going to be easy. I know my girl and she'll do whatever she has to and not complain at all. We'll probably have to make her take it easy. Her zest for life is amazing. She's one that the more you tell her she can't do something the more she wants to prove to you that she can and she will. Cassie will meet and surpass every goal she sets for herself. She will enrich every life she ever touches she already does. I see a lot of Timmy in her...Oh god, I still haven't told Doug about Timmy. The time just isn't right yet...soon.

Chapter XVIII

(the awakening)

Lost in my own thoughts I almost didn't realize that Cassie's little hand had begun to twitch. She's waking up! "Hi beautiful girl, how are you feeling?" Her vision is a bit hazy and she still has the oxygen mask on but I see her big beautiful smile peek out past the mask. I love staring into those baby blues. The eyes are the window to the soul and Cassie's eyes are deep and full of love and wonder. She expresses her inner most feeling through her eyes. How I love this little girl, I'd give my life for her. My precious gift from God that is what my Cassie is. What's wrong baby I wonder as her brows furrow up? "Where's Timmy mommy? Did we get him out of the well?" My eyes flew to Doug, all the color drained from his face. He looks like he was hit with a ton of brick. His eyes dart from Cassie to me and back to Cassie. The confusion is very apparent. I don't know what to do. Doug left the room, I'm torn because Cassie needs me but right now Doug needs me more. "Cassie honey, mommy will be right outside the room. I have to talk to daddy for a minute ok?" I pray she will somehow understand. She just smiles and I know it's ok to leave.

I have to get out of the room it is too small, I can't breathe...oh my god. My mind is going in a million different directions. Why did Cassie mention Timmy? She never talks about Timmy unless Faye brings him up. Why now? I don't understand. The look on Faye's face was shock and disbelief. I'm so very confused right now, I felt like someone punched me in the gut all the wind somehow left my body. Deep in thought I don't realize that Faye has come out of Cassie's room and has taken my hand and is guiding me to the bench. "Sit she says...please." So I numbingly sit barely aware of my surroundings. "Doug, when I found Cassie she wasn't alone, are you listening to me? When I got to the bottom of the well...Doug I found our son, I found Timmy." I looked at Faye in disbelief and anger. "You-you found Timmy at the bottom of the well? You didn't think that was important information that I had a right to know? Faye he was ...is-is my son too." I knew Doug was lashing out so I just continued..."Yes, Cassie was huddled up next to him clutching his teddy bear. He helped her Doug. I think he gave her comfort, took away her fear and pain." Wh-where is he now? Did you leave him in the well he snarled?" Faye calmly answered back, "No Doug, I packed up all his stuff and he is at home wrapped up in my coat. I couldn't leave him down there...Timmy is at home. Cassie talked to him and she drew strength from his presence. Officer Jess came to see us while you were in surgery with Cassie and he said something that touched me deeply and I want to share it with you. It gave me peace and I think in time it will do the same for you." He said... "He may have met his death in that well, but he was never alone. Take some comfort in that. Edna has been taking care of his spirit all these years. What you found was just the shell. Your little boy is in heaven. When Cassie needed him he was there to help her. His presence alone took away her fear. His teddy bear comforted her. She was not alone at the bottom of that well she had an angel by her side." At that moment the anger left and nestled in my wife's arms I cried. The tears that I had been afraid to shed came out like torrents. I let all the emotion out the fear, the pain, and the wretched loneliness. And the guilt, my god the guilt came pouring out. I forgot my son and he fell down a well and died alone and scared because of me. I cried until there were no more tears left in me. Would I ever heal from this? Lost in my self-pity and self-loathing I felt a heart wrenching pain in the pit of my stomach. I finally let myself grieve and mourn my son. Faye just held me as I rocked back and forth. She grieved a long time ago and she knew that someday I would too and that day was today. She just held me and ran her fingers through my hair until finally the tears stopped and I looked into her eyes. This was the beginning of my process of grief. It was as if I had just lost my son all over again. Maybe in the back of my mind I never let myself feel because I prayed that he would come home. Well now he is home...my angel is home and we can finally put him to rest.

Cassie stayed in the hospital for a week. Doug never left her side. Somehow the tides had turned and I was the strong one. For now, anyway, we had yet to go home and put Timmy to rest. Doug had yet to see his son after all these years. Realty had just begun to set in for Doug. Cassie talked about Timmy like he was her friend. It was hard and comforting at the same time. She still wanted Doug to explain to her why Timmy was so small. Wasn't he her older brother? Doug wasn't ready to face it yet and would quickly change the subject.

Chapter XIX

(the recovery)

Officer Jess came to see Cassie. He brought her coloring books and ice cream. He sat and talked with her while Doug and I would go freshen up in the doctor's lounge. Doug wasn't ready to go home yet so we bought toothbrushes and toiletries and lived in scrubs for the entire week. At least some of the nurses took pity on me and brought me real shampoo and a hairbrush. We were there as long as Cassie was and that was that. Everyday Cassie got stronger and the infection in her blood started to go away. That's why we were still in the hospital, her hip was healing nicely but the infection from the stagnant water among other things was an uphill battle. But slowly Cassie was winning and getting better. The Specialist told us that by the end of the week or early next week Cassie would be able to do the rest of her recuperation at home. She will have to start the physical therapy for her hip and leg but that will be slow and steady. By this time next month, she should be able to walk unassisted with crutches. If all goes well, she will be walking on a cane in a few months and then the sky is the limit! Cassie grinned from ear-to-ear at the news. She kind of liked her scar it made her feel important and cool and everyone always fussed over her. She was the center of attention and she liked it. Mom had always given her lots of attention and she knew that she was dad's favorite. This was somehow different though, her hip hurt for sure but she managed and never complained. She wasn't looking forward to trying to walk because she knew it was going to hurt. Twice a day a nurse came in and stretched and rubbed her leg and hip to keep it from seizing up on her. At least that's what the nurse said when Cassie asked her why she was doing that. Of course, Cassie had no idea what that meant. She made a mental note to ask daddy the next time she saw him. Cassie had noticed that daddy seemed sad lately. He always had a smile for her and some type of treat but when he thought Cassie wasn't paying attention, she could see the pain in his eyes. He looked lost...not lost like she was in the woods but somehow he looked lost like he didn't know what to do. The best description she could give was like when her friend Gary from down their street lost his puppy. That's the sad look that daddy projected. She decided that she was going to give him an extra hug today. Daddy always said that when he wasn't feeling good or had a hard day at work Cassie hugs were the best medicine. So today she was going to take care of daddy and give him some extra medicine.

Chapter XX

(Doug's mourning)

I'm trying to get past Faye and Cassie's news about Timmy. He's been gone for so long why is it affecting me like this? Long ago I resigned myself to the fact that Timmy was dead. I think it is just hard to hear and imagine how my son died. I felt so responsible...who forgets their young child at home? Faye said he must have lived a little while in that well because he was leaning against the wall hugging his knees when she found him down there. I can imagine the fear he felt. As a parent you want to protect your children and to know that Timmy died scared and all alone is just too much. I have put off going to the house. I don't know if I can bear seeing my son like that. I know Faye and Cassie are worried, sometimes out of the corner of my eye I see Faye studying my face. Cassie is no dummy either. I have to get past this if not for myself then for my wife and daughter. I just don't know how. I think I'll go for a walk.

I found a bench on the hospital grounds that was secluded from all the other benches. The sun was out but even when I looked up, I couldn't feel the sunlight all I felt was a cold numb feeling in the pit of my stomach. I just sat and stared into nothing. I didn't notice Officer Jess sit down next to me. "Hey Doug, he said...how are you doing? How is Cassie?" I mumbled something to him, honestly I just wanted him to go away so I could wallow in my grief and self-pity. But he continued to talk. I'm not even sure what he said until he mentioned the well. Jess had found the well where my son lost his life, and my daughter almost did. I hadn't really thought of the well as something tangible until now. I perked up and listened now in earnest. "Doug I found the well he said and I went down into it he continued...And now the well is gone." He destroyed it and made it so that no one adult or child can ever fall into it again. I was happy about this but sad at the same time. I wanted to see where my son spent his last moments of life and now I could not. "I thought it might help you to see where Timmy died...he continued." Something about pictures...when you are ready to see them." With that I just got up and walked away. Jess didn't try to follow me he just watched me walk away.

Before I knew it I was in the car and driving. I didn't have a destination in mind I just drove aimlessly (or so I thought.) I rounded a familiar corner that I really never came to much anymore. Somehow my subconscious led me to the graveyard where mom was buried. A twinge of guilt passed through me, I seemed to always find one excuse or another not to visit her. Yet, somehow here I was. I knelt at her grave and poured out my soul. I told her how Cassie had gotten lost and fell down the well, I told her how I had looked and looked and could not find her. Finally, I told her that my beautiful

Faye had braved the woods and found our Cassie. Then my shoulders slumped, and I told her how she not only found Cassie she also found Timmy. While I was telling her all of this something hit me. I remembered Mom's last days, I remembered how she insisted on sitting outside (even on the coldest days) the realization hit me like a mac truck. Mom knew, she knew Timmy was in the woods. She talked to him every day...I remember now. Faye was right, Timmy wasn't alone. I jumped up; it was like a weight was lifted from my shoulders. I had to tell Faye and I needed to hug my Cassie. I got in the car and raced back to the hospital. I knew now I could finally put Timmy to rest. I had to find Jess, he had said something about the well and pictures. First thing was first though I had to go back to the hospital to the family that loved me. I whipped into the parking lot and took the stairs two at a time until I reached Cassie's ward. I threw open the door and ran over and hugged the two most important people in my life. Faye was startled and Cassie was laughing, me I was crying. I told Faye where I had gone and what I had done, she just quietly listened. I told her that while I was pouring my heart out to mom I finally realized that Timmy was not alone. Mom was there with him, she gave him comfort and took away the fear. Timmy was not alone in a watery grave he was in heaven with Edna. I always knew they had a bond but I guess I really had no idea how deep it ran until now. I told Faye that now I could put Timmy to rest. We hugged and she brushed the hair out of my face and kissed my forehead. We were going to survive this. Even in death Timmy had taken care of Cassie just as Enda had taken care of him.

The weekend passed quickly and Cassie got stronger. The rosy color returned to her cheeks and finally the Specialist gave us the green light to take her home. She said her goodbyes to all the nurses, and we packed her up and took her home. She had a long road to complete recovery but together the three of us would do it. When we pulled up to the house Faye put her hand on my arm. Faye knew what waited for them in the house. Before they had taken Cassie to the hospital, she had laid Timmy out on his bed and placed his raggedy teddy bear next to him. Doug assured her he could do this and with that they entered the house. Doug asked that he go see Timmy on his own and Faye respected his wishes. Faye took Cassie into her own room to put away her things and tuck her into bed. Cassie was better but she still tired easily so they had to make sure she got plenty of rest. After Faye tucked her in bed, she sat next to her and took her in her arms and softly sang to her as she ran her fingers softly through Cassie's hair until her daughter was asleep. Faye tucked Miss Bunny under the covers and quietly moved to the chair where she could watch her daughter peacefully sleep and give Doug time with his son.

With a deep breath Doug entered Timmy's room. He knew every inch of that room but now somehow it was different to him. He came close to the bed and looked down at his son. Timmy was so small, just like Faye when he looked down he thought he'd see a skeleton but all he saw was his beautiful boy. He gingerly sat on the edge of the bed and wept. There lay his son, yes he knew he was dead. But he was still his little boy. His heart broke when he thought of all the things that Timmy would never experience. He'd never go to school, he'd never graduate. He ached for his son because he knew he'd never fall in love and get married...But one thing he knew was that Timmy was loved and now Timmy was home. Doug got up and left the room.

Later that night Faye and Doug had a very difficult conversation. They had to plan Timmy's funeral. They decided that they would bury him next to Edna. It was surreal to Doug because although Faye cried, she remained stoic and strong. She could finally put her little boy to rest. Somehow that brought her comfort. There would be hard days ahead, but they would face them as a family. In a way their family was complete now and that brought them a sense of peace. They went to bed that night and held each other deep into the night. Neither one spoke, they were lost in their own thoughts. Tomorrow they would make the necessary phone calls and do what had to be done. Sleep finally came and calm dreamless sleep. Morning came and they just went through the motions...breakfast, coffee and then the calls began. It took about an hour to arrange everything but then it was done. The funeral would be Monday and the viewing would be tomorrow. The Funeral parlor wanted to come collect

Timmy so they could prepare him. Faye and I decided that we would take him there ourselves. We got Cassie ready and carefully bundled Timmy up (not forgetting his teddy bear) and made the sorrowful trip to the Funeral parlor. We surrendered him to the caretaker who assured us they would take good care of him, and we picked out his casket. A small blue casket with a soft velvet lining. We had his name engraved on it and Faye wrote a poem that would be said during the service. We chose a headstone in the shape of an angel. Everything was set for us to bury our son. Officer Jess asked if he could have the honor along with Doug to carry the casket as a pall bearer. It was all set...it was all done. We gathered up our daughter and went home.

The Funeral...

Beautiful Faye stood next to Timmy's casket as they gently lowered him down into his grave...She lovingly gazed at her son and read this poem.

Timmy
I miss you my son every day
Precious memories of you are all that I have
I hope one day my heart will mend
A smile in lieu of a tear
It is ever so hard my son to finally let you go

So God I'll lend you my son if only for a little while
Please shelter him with love
Please comfort all his fear
We'll brave the waves of grief that I know will come
You took him much sooner than planned
I will struggle and try to understand

Slumber deep my son you are finally home
You didn't deserve what befell you
Peaceful and free from pain
I love you my son

With that Timmy was lowered into the ground, his final resting place. Sweet sorrow but peace...Faye and Doug and Cassie each dropped a single rose upon the mound of dirt and sod that held Timmy. Doug scooped Cassie up in his arms held his wife's hand and turned and walked away. Timmy was safe now next to Edna...It was finally time, time to go home.

The End

ABOUT THE AUTHOR

I am a military brat, I was born in Hawaii and raised in a town called Waianae. I joined the Army right out of High School and after Basic Training, my permanent duty station was the USAMEDDAC in Bremerhaven West Germany. I had met and fell in love with my soulmate during High School. We married young, and it did not work out at that time.

Life goes on, I had four beautiful daughters with two other great people. Your heart is a funny thing, I guess I just never gave my heart to either one of them completely. How can give you give something that someone else already has? I honestly thought that I would never see my soulmate again. Life had other plans for us though and thirty years later he found me on LinkedIn. We have since remarried and life is amazing with." My Tights!"

After the military, my life was good for a while until I got sick and after many surgeries my "self-therapy" was writing this book. All my pain, fear of the unknown and frustrations went into the pages of this book. I believe that all fictional writing starts with a little bit of truth. Here is my truth. Thank you...Jax

CPSIA information can be obtained
at www.ICGtesting.com
Printed in the USA
BVHW031548260223
659226BV00008B/685